Th

They Don't Roost in Some

Random Coop

in Another State.

And other Short Stories

The Winner's Anthology

For the

2009 Christian Writing Contest

Sponsored by

Athanatos Christian Ministries

ATHANATOS
PUBLISHING GROUP

Athanatos Christian Ministries is proud to release this anthology containing the winners' entries of its first annual Christian writing contest. As an apologetics organization, ACM designed the contest with the desire to raise up Christian authors who could reflect the Christian worldview through written narrative. With so many voices influencing opinions, hearts, and attitudes, and the stakes as high as they are, ACM believes that it is more important than ever to have Christians involved in the conversation.

ACM would like to thank all of the judges and sponsors for their help in making this contest possible, and of course Jesus Christ, the one at the center of the Grand Narrative that we are all caught up within. Our stories, in comparison, are mere dim shadows, but we pray that God will use them to guide others into a relationship with He who is the Author of All.

To read the 2009 winning entries online and learn more about future contests, please visit:
www.christianwritingcontest.com

In Christ,

Anthony Horvath
Executive Director
Athanatos Christian Ministries, Inc.

Athanatos Christian Ministries

is proud to present the 2009

C.S. Lewis Award

to

Michael Pape

Irving, TX

1st Place

(Category: 19 and up)

Bio: Michael Pape grew up in Wauwatosa, Wisconsin, which taught him the value of hard work and moon boots. He likes cheese and dogs, and dislikes raw onions and cats. He can currently be found fixing computers or writing crazy stuff in either Irving, TX or an unspecified location in Wisconsin, depending on when you're reading this. His web page is: www.epthnation.com

Those Chickens, They Don't Roost in Some Random Coop in Another State.

by Michael Pape

copyright 2009, All Rights Reserved

The neighbor's cat was determined and fearless, and it was now balancing itself on Derrick Hearst's backyard fence. He believed the cat's name to be Sprickles, but he almost certainly had that wrong. Sprinkles? Sparkles? Oh, he supposed it could also be their other cat, Tushka. It's impossible to tell two similar cats apart when you don't care about either. At least this explained the dirty little clumps of cat fur he kept finding in his yard.

On most other days, Derrick wouldn't be staring out his kitchen window at 9am. He would be at the office, making sure the people who wished to stab him in the back got preemptively stabbed before they could brandish their knives. But today, he called in. Threw in the towel. Raised the white flag. Quit before he began. And why?

Because of a bad dream.

The cat carefully prowled along the top of the fence for a few seconds, then stopped. Its gaze scanned the yard like a spotlight on a guard tower — forward and back, forward and back. Derrick loved to see animals hunt, even if this wasn't exactly the wild. It was searching for something, but what?

———

His stunned state was caused by more than just a dream — the seeds for this were planted a week before, during a "non-mandatory teamwork and self-improvement exercise" held by his employer. It was billed the Weekend of Hypnosis and Beer, and it was held at the Twilight Hills Retreat Center, a spa/lodge/holistic (read: wacked-out) wellness complex 2 hours outside of town in the lovely Clackamas Valley. The stated purpose of the weekend was to eliminate all self-defeating thoughts from the attendees' heads. He agreed to do it because he always attended any work-related event, especially the non-mandatory ones. They were all part of the game. Plus, everybody has self-defeating thoughts, right? If hypnosis and beer are all it takes to defeat them, then why not partake?

There was a shuttle from the office to the THRC for any interested attendees, but he decided to take his new BMW instead. I mean, come on — why go to a work event if you're not going to show off a little? He hadn't paid 50 grand for a totally impractical little car just to leave it at home during showtime. The weekend was being run by the Twilight Hills staff, all of whom all had a decidedly hippie vibe about them, even while wearing polos and khakis. There wasn't one male THRC person without a ponytail. This was the first bad sign. The next one came when he was handed the Schedule of Events, which was packed with things like "Group Meditations" and "Nature Walks." There seemed to be very little hypnosis planned, and even less beer. He wondered why he was even there, but he recognized that as the kind of self-defeating thought this weekend was supposed to be about eliminating. Of course, because he was Derrick Hearst, go-getter, he ended up throwing himself full-bore into these activities without thinking about the consequences first. The Boss, after all, might be watching, and his bespectacled eyes appreciated constant enthusiasm for whatever the company thought was worth being enthusiastic about, no matter how inane or pointless.

The first night they all got together in a big flourescently-lit room and did team-building exercises. Derrick *hated* these things. It was like they were baiting the negative thoughts out of him. After what seemed like hours of Getting to Know Your Teammates, they each went to their own rooms *without any beer at all*. That was such a downer. Derrick wanted to talk to some of his office-mates —

Morrison from sales, that Amanda chick from Logistics, the albino HR guy who always wanted to discuss fantasy baseball — about how lame Friday night was, but didn't dare. If word got back to some of his enemies in the office, the ones that wanted his job and the jobs he coveted, they would surely bring it up to the Boss, and that would result in a big black mark of uncertainty being placed on him like a scarlet letter. It would be on his permanent record. He hadn't worked this hard for five of his best years to be brought down by some non-mandatory work activity, no matter how lame it was.

The next day brought with it the promised hypnosis, and significantly more beer than Derrick thought was possible. Because of the beer, and possibly the hypnosis, he didn't remember much. He remembered getting up at 7am and going for a wonderful, pore-opening run in a majestic valley. He remembered taking a shower and rushing down to the kitchen just in time for the end of breakfast, which turned out to be runny eggs and toast with some funky-tasting hippie-produced jam. At 10am the group meditation started, and he remembered everyone lying flat on their backs on the same kinds of mats he once used during nap time in Kindergarten. He remembered starting to space out, and thinking that hypnosis is just being really sleepy. He remembered being instructed to find his "safe place," or place in his mind where he could be safe and feel like everything was super great. For that, he chose to imagine his old college frat house. He didn't remember his reasoning in picking that place (since he hadn't thought of it in…like forever), but he remembered mentally walking up to the red wooden door on the front of the house, shoving it open (it always stuck), and stepping into the foyer. He remembered it being unusually warm inside the frat house in his mind, so he decided to go into the hall and change the thermostat, again in his mind. He was getting a little bored with the exercise at this point, and just needed something to do. Moving from the foyer to his right, he strolled down the two steps into the main party room. The hallway was on the other side of the couch. He remembered it being really tedious to continue imagining the process of walking step-by-step, so he flew over the couches in the middle of the room and into the darkness of the back hallway. There was a bright blue light coming from under the door at the end of the hall, but that was the only thing Derrick could see. He couldn't even see the hallway walls, and it felt like the darkness was crushing him.

He then remembered waking up to the sound of a clanging bell being enthusiastically wrung by one of the ponytail guys. It was 5pm in the evening. He had "slept" right through lunch, as had (apparently) all his office-mates. When he awoke, he was greeted by the sound of rushing water and the smell of bacon. He remembered being totally confused and disoriented, and thinking that he was still back in college. The rushing water turned out to be a CD the hippies were playing, and the bacon turned out to be, well, bacon. It was dinnertime.

He remembered sitting down at the long supper table and seeing two giant kegs on a stand at the far end of the room — one of LaBatt Blue and one of Molson. He remembered thinking that the hippies must be Canadian, which actually explained a lot. He was very excited at the first appearance of beer, even the crappy Canadian kind. He went over to the keg stand and poured himself a frosty one, then sat back down. He vaguely remembered drinking and eating that night, but for some reason he felt like he was having a meal in his old frat house, as if the hypnosis session and the meal were mixed together in his mind. He didn't remember anything after dinner, either – the scene dissolves as he's drinking Molson at the dinner table, and resumes the next morning with him waking up in a pool of sweat.

On Sunday, he asked Morrison from sales — the only one in the company he felt he could really trust with such a question — about the previous night, and Morrie indicated that ol' Derrick had been the life of the party. There was apparently lots of karaoke and bad drunken dancing involved, and possibly a 10pm "nature stumble." He assumed he had gotten drunk and blacked out while on his feet, and he expected memories of that night to come flooding back as they always did in these situations, but they never came. That night, and most of that day, has remained an impenetrable mystery to Derrick, even after Morrison forwarded him a link to an internet video featuring Derrick dancing with the ugliest life-sized clown statue in the world and singing that inane "In the Year 2525" song. He didn't remember any of what he saw on that video. He had been drunk before (too many times to count, especially in college) but never had he been so out-of-it that he permanently forgot a memorable shindig.

The cat stood motionless in a dead crouch on top of the wooden fence. It seemed to be staring very intently at the one tree in his backyard, the giant spruce he desperately needed to have trimmed. It stayed in the crouch for at least 30 seconds, patiently waiting for something. The top of the fence was no more than two inches wide, and the cat's sense of balance was quite impressive. It was trying to become, for all intents and purposes, part of the fence.

Calling in sick was a brand-new experience for Derrick, and as he was about to dial the office, he realized he had no idea how to do it. What does one say? He knew about the proverbial pretend-coughing and such, but didn't know how much of a ruse was necessary. He had a bigger problem, though — if he called in sick, people would undoubtedly view this as extremely out-of-character for him, and assume he was either a) on his deathbed, or b) having a nervous breakdown (a la what happened to Dzelzkalns last year). It didn't matter that b) was probably right; what mattered is that there would be a chance that the Boss would send someone to his house to check on him. Even if nobody came, he would at the very least have to field several "concerned" phone calls disguised as work questions. He needed to have his story straight. If he claimed illness, they would send a doctor and the jig would be up (more likely, the doctor would diagnose it as "stress," which would effectively end his career advancement because he would now be "unable to deal with the pressure" or whatever). However, if he said he just needed a day off, he would prove himself unreliable on a day-to-day basis, and that would be that. He could see no way out of this conundrum, besides going to work. And since going to work with those people was definitely not an option, at least not today...

He calmly dialed the office number and spoke his pre-planned script to the albino from HR, the one that would most likely shoot down his rising corporate star. He went with illness, the kind that has served derelict workers for decades — sore throat, sore muscles, probably highly contagious. He even did a fake cough, mostly out of guilt. He was going to see the doctor, and might be in later if everything looked okay. He hung up the phone and stared straight ahead at nothing in particular. After all he had done for that company and that Boss, they owed him at least one mulligan.

—

He continued to stare out the window at the cat on the fence, but he wasn't thinking about the cat. His mind wandered to the dream he had experienced earlier, the one that had set his rocker off its hinges and out the door. It was getting fuzzier with each passing minute, as these things do, but he vividly remembered the end of the dream. In it, he walked through the glass doors that separated his company's office from the rest of the Brubaker Building. Everything looked the same as real life, except for a couple inches of freshly-fallen snow on the floor and the cubicles. He was wearing one of his normal everyday suits, and was shivering from the cold. He crunched his way through the snow down the hall past cubicle row, and noticed that nobody else was there. He walked left through the open doorway to his own personal office, and suddenly found himself outside in a blowing snowstorm. There was a woman in a white hooded sweatshirt about 20 feet ahead of him holding a shovel, and he trudged up to her and tapped her on the shoulder. She turned and looked at him. He vaguely recognized her face, but could not think of her name. (What was her name again? No. Just NO!)

The mystery woman smiled, dropped her shovel, and whispered, "On to the next thing."

He awoke, not knowing where or who he was. It was 4:42 in the morning. This rang a bell in his head, and he just lay there and let reality re-coalesce around him. He didn't want to think about the woman in white, or 442, or the snowstorm, or the dream (No. Just NO!). Staring up at the ceiling, he thought about fantasy baseball. He discussed with himself for at least 30 minutes the possible merits of trading for a different backup catcher, then went on to mentally tweak his outfield. He got scared a little when he thought of the consequences of losing one of his starters, such as that unhittable stud Cole Hamels, to injury. Two hours later, he got up and took a shower. The thought of going to work (Just NO!) made him nauseous, all of a sudden. He blamed the Canadian hippies, but it didn't take.

He made some coffee and the deceptive phone call. He read the paper and listened to some talk radio. It was 9am. What do people who call in sick *do* all day anyway? He missed the office, and with it the habitual clawing for that golden ring that so consumed every minute of his days. So why was he watching this cat become one with a fence again? And why had he made his coffee so Irish this morning?

Because...(Just NO!)

—

The cat still stood in the same exact place. It had been at least 10 minutes since the cat stopped moving. Derrick could tell it was still watching the tree, and had figured out that it was actually the birds inside the tree that the feline predator was watching. He counted at least 20 brown and black birds in its ample supply of branches, most of whom were just hanging out and chirping. Some of the black ones were making noises that sounded like electrical equipment short-circuiting. He hated those oily birds and their gosh-awful racket.

Something must have spooked the birds, because instantaneously the tree emptied, pouring black and brown blobs into the air towards the fence. Derrick thought at first that the cat would be knocked off the fence like Humpty-Dumpty, but the birds all flew over and past the cat in their hysterical race to escape. The cat waited silently, crouching even lower, and what happened next forced coffee out of Derrick's mouth and nose and onto his Parisian silk bathrobe.

The last bird out of the tree was a brown one, looking bigger and plumper than any of the others. In an instantaneous burst of motion, the cat pounced off the fence directly toward the path of the flying brown bird. It had compensated for the brown blob's speed and acceleration, and if the bird noticed the flying cat it was far too late;

the bird was carried by inertia into the waiting claws of the feline missile, and the two small animals crashed to the ground in a explosion of fur, feathers, and squawking. As the coffee hit the bathrobe, Derrick looked around as if to say, "Did anyone else but me see THAT?" Looking back at the ground, he saw that the impact of hitting the lawn had caused the cat to let go of its avian prey, and the scared plump brown victim was flapping its wings in a panic in order to get away from the momentarily stunned cat. The predator took a split second to roll to its feet, and shot off towards the bird. At first, it was making up ground, but even fat brown birds can eventually out-fly a ground-ridden cat. Eventually, the bird got high enough in the air to clear the fence, and the cat stopped and began walking in circles. It was looking up in the air, and now had an obvious limp.

The cat deserved the limp for trying something so rash, stupid, and unnecessary, thought Derrick. There were probably Tender Vittles waiting at home in a dish — didn't the cat know that? It squeezed its little furry body under the fence with great difficulty, hind legs clawing at the ground in a desperate push. There was just enough space for it to smush its bones in-between the fence and the grass below, and it was tearing a hole in his lawn. Stupid cat.

—

As Tushka or Sprickles' hindquarters slowly disappeared, Derrick looked down at the brown stain on his robe and wondered what could get coffee out of Parisian silk. Amazingly, the shock of cat vs. bird had taken the starch out of his malaise, and he now found himself able to think semi-clearly. The cat may have been a gift from God, sent to snap him out of his mental prison and help him face whatever he had to face. (No. Just NO!)

(Maybe.)

(Ok, FINE. Have it your way.)

If there was guilt inside him for what had happened to Abbie Rehfeldt, it was time to deal with it. Drinking himself into oblivion during hypnosis weekend didn't stop this, and neither did pleading ignorance. It's obvious that things like the bad dream would keep happening until he found a way to be rid of them. He couldn't afford to miss any more days of work. This had to end now. Only a clear-headed man could achieve what Derrick wanted to achieve in life, so it was time to cleanse his head. And he knew a possible way to do it. Hoping for a lucky break, he pulled his laptop out of his briefcase, set it on the dining room table, and attempted to open the lid. His hands were shaking so much he was unable to pop the latch.

—

He really didn't remember much about Abbie, since he only met her once, and that was over nine years ago. He couldn't recall anything about her face, but always remembered she had jet-black straight hair that went down to the middle of her back. What he thought of most were the things she told him during their conversation at the beginning of his very first frat party. She was a freshman, just like him. She grew up in some crazy cult in Alabama that she literally had to escape from, like through underground tunnels. She hadn't seen her parents in four years, because they had disowned her. It was a really heavy conversation, filled with the sorts of things you'd discuss at the end of a party, rather than at the beginning.

So when the slimeball Steve Sanderson took him aside and handed him a vial of some clear liquid with the numbers "442″ on it and told Derrick to drop it in her drink, that this was part of the initiation process, and that everybody does it before they get into the Brotherhood of Alpha Mu Rho, it was quite disappointing. He thought she was pretty cool, a fact that always bothered him on those few occasions he thought back to the events of that night. This wasn't some dumb sorority girl we were talking about here — this girl had substance. It wasn't even clear how she was able to get in the party in the first place, since she apparently didn't come with anyone. Abbie was just a naive alone girl trying to make some friends. For that mistake, she was victimized in a way that Derrick couldn't allow himself to think about.

She left to go to the bathroom. His eyes and Slimeball Steve's met. He looked down at the vial. *Everybody does it. Part of the initiation process. I need to do this to get on to the next thing.* God, all those thoughts, and many more, went through his head. He was trying to convince himself. He confirmed that Steve was still looking at him, emptied his brain, and felt a flood of something enter him — Confidence? Power? The Devil? Whatever it was, it got past all the mental barriers he had, and he coldly opened the vial and poured it right in her nearly-full beer glass. Now not only Steve but Brett "The Plow" Wilkinson and Terry Leonard and like 12 other Brotherhood members were smiling at him. Some were nodding approvingly. He took his finger and stirred Abbie's beer. She came back and smiled at him. She fricking *smiled* at him, after that. She sat down and asked why he was sweating.

It is precisely at this point that the memory fades. Thinking about it always made him sick to his stomach (No. Just NO!), so he tried his best to forget it and get on with his life. He had succeeded for nearly nine years. He hadn't thought of Abbie Rehfeldt at all since he landed his current job, and with it the girlfriends, the house, the BMW, and the stress. He made *one* mistake in his life, and he couldn't get away from it. The whole thing wasn't even his fault! I mean, Steve gave him the vial and made him use it. It wasn't Derrick's plan. So why did he feel so guilty?

—

Ever since making the transition from sales to management, Derrick had found the internet to be an invaluable tool in evaluating and understanding the people who worked for him. It always amazed him that people would put personal details, likes, dislikes, and dreams out there where anyone, even their enemies, could find it. He needed to clear his conscience once and for all. Surely Abbie Rehfeldt had an internet presence. Surely she would be a successful writer, or banker, or something. Surely this one thoughtless act hadn't totally derailed her life. A desperate hope filled his soul as he finally popped the latch and got the laptop open.

He typed her name into the Google search box and pressed enter. It was entirely possible that she got married, and now had a different name, but he had no way of knowing that. The first result that came up under "Abbie Rehfeldt" was a ZPlace page, one of those social networking sites where people typically put too much information about themselves. This might be it, he thought. He clicked on the link, and came to Abbie Rehfeldt's ZPlace page. This particular Abbie Rehfeldt had customized her page with a black background and some blinking crucifixes. There were tiny blinking Jesuses all over the screen. At the top of the page was a picture of a raven-haired girl who looked like the one he remembered from nine years ago. This was definitely her, the Abbie Rehfeldt he once met. There didn't seem to be much on her site — some generic comments from various people he didn't know, the one picture, the blinking background, and that was pretty much it. She didn't even have any hometown listed. Derrick's hopes faded, but he did notice the page stretched past the bottom of the screen.

Scrolling down and scanning her "notes" section brought everything into focus. He couldn't believe what he was seeing at first. Was this a joke? He looked away, and looked again. It was still there. In all caps, the note's title screamed TO DERRICK HEARST. The walls of his home started to spin counterclockwise around him, and his field of vision was reduced to a small circle around those three words. After a few seconds of spinning he succumbed to the encroaching darkness and slumped completely off his chair...

...And was back in the frat house hallway, facing the back door just like during the group meditation. This time, however, he slowly walked toward the door (instead of running away in terror for hours). It was open a crack, and the light coming from behind it was a burning bluish-white. Derrick pushed open the door and was greeted by a rush of cold air. The room was filled with falling snow, and before him stood the woman from his dream, the one with the white hooded sweatshirt. She took down the hood, but she didn't have to. He knew it was Abbie. Who else would it be? She smiled at him, the same smile he saw after his treacherous act. He started to cry.

"Why are you crying?"

"Because...it's all so horrible."

"Horrible? You haven't even faced it yet."

"What do you mean? I came into the room. I know what I did."

"Do you? Why is it snowing?"

Derrick thought about this for a bit. He didn't know. He was sure he didn't want to know. The stern-faced White Abbie held out her hands in front of her, and cradled inside them was a tiny, twinkling snow globe. The dream got loud and black immediately, and he was forcibly ejected from his own head.

He heard frenzied yelling, and his sprawled-out body sat up in an instant. He was sitting on the floor of the kitchen, and the yelling he heard was coming from his own mouth. With its ceasing came the surrounding sounds of the mundane — the refrigerator was humming, the birds outside were making friendly little chirps, his wall clock was methodically ticking, and he was breathing heavily. The chair out of which he fell was directly in front of his outstretched legs. The concept of standing up didn't quite process yet, so he just sat there and let his senses lead him. The distracting smell of coffee was coming from his robe, his throat felt tingly and sore, and his cheeks were damp with tears. His eyes went up to his laptop computer, sitting on the table. Oh, yeah. TO DERRICK HURST.

—

Less than five minutes after the 18-year-old Derrick Hurst had done the dirty deed, even before Abbie showed signs of feeling whatever effects were in store for her, he got sick and excused himself from the impending act. He didn't want to hear any of what would be going on in that back room, so he went outside and vomited over the porch railing into the bushes below. There was a recliner on the porch, so he collapsed into it and stared out into the night sky above campus. It was an absolutely gorgeous fall night. A bit chilly, but gorgeous. Next to the recliner was a small wooden table with a snow globe on it, which he picked up and began to turn back and forth and upside down. The snowman inside stared at him with two black pinhole eyes, and it was never not smiling. The little flakes floated up and down in the water, making it look like the stereotypical winter scene it was intended to be. Between the hypnotic globe and the comfortable recliner, Derrick was able to relax a bit and take stock of what had just happened.

He never thought of himself as a criminal, but he had committed a heinous crime, one he could go to jail for. One he *should* go to jail for. This really was beyond the pale. He was now a real-live criminal, thanks to the Brotherhood. They owed him now, big time. What if she told people? He knew the Brotherhood would stick together, but that might not deter her from calling the authorities. If he could just...

This was ludicrous. He was a criminal. It didn't matter if she told anyone — the truth would always be that he did this terrible thing to another human being. And his first thought is "What if she tells people?" What the hell kind of man was he anyway? It was that Slimeball Steve's fault. He had made Derrick an unwilling accomplice, and now the Brotherhood and Derrick stood together in mud and blood. Maybe that's why they have initiations like this in the first place. Nothing binds people together like a secret that's too evil to tell, right? What kind of people had he just attached himself to?

On the other hand, he was now definitely a Brother, which marked the culmination of this stage in his life plan. He needed this. Being a Brother would mean connections, a probable good job, prestige, and an incalculable number of tremendous potential experiences. He had to do what he just did, if he wanted his life to work out in a superior way. Sometimes tough moral choices just needed to be made by men of action. Would the admiration of friends and family make up for the guilt of destroying that poor girl's life? Probably, eventually.

So as the snowman fell prey to an intense snowstorm which pelted him from all sides and turned his life upside down, Derrick decided that this Just Didn't Happen. He would not think of it again. If someone brought it up, he would act like he didn't know what that person was talking about. She might accuse him, but admitting it wouldn't help anyone. The Brotherhood were the only ones who knew the truth, and they would never tell. It wasn't over and done with, because it was a non-event.

He put the globe down, walked to his dorm room, and slept his sleep.

—

And now as he sat alone on the dining room floor of his four-bedroom ranch-style house, he realized that everything he had, he owed to Abbie Rehfeldt. If he hadn't made that bad choice, it was possible, even probable, that the Brotherhood wouldn't have accepted him. That would have meant no internship with the Plow's dad, and no job offer from Duke's family friend, and no experience which led to a job with his current company, and no BMW or nice house or closets full of suits or hot girlfriends or membership at the Club. He might have turned out just as successful, but probably not. In any case, he used *that* to become *this*, and he therefore owed it all to her. There's guilt, and then there's the kind of guilt that has nowhere to go, and so it just seeps into every cell of one's body and stays there, never moving, waiting to pounce at an opportune moment. It had measured exactly the right time, and jumped when Derrick saw his own name on his victim's ZPlace page. It was all too much, and it wasn't going away. The parade of "on to the next thing" had ended. There would be no next thing, anymore.

The last thing on earth Derrick wanted to do was read that note. He wanted to get up, go to work, push the guilt back down his gullet, and get back to his life. But he owed her this. This was about her, Abbie Rehfeldt, the real human. He was led to her — he didn't know how, or why, but there was definitely a set-up involved — and coming this far was pointless if he didn't go the rest of the way. So he crawled up from the floor and slid into the chair in front of the computer. The screensaver was up, and the words "Failure Is Not an Option" floated by in 3-D. That platitude seemed so…completely dead, now. He hit a key and the blinking crucifixes were back. He closed his eyes, and tears formed as the afterimage of crucified saviors filled his entire field of view. She was a real person, and the event was a real event, and these were facts he couldn't bear for much longer. He clicked on the note, which brought him to a new page.

The note said:

Derrick,
i don't know why, but i feel the need to do this. you'll probably never read it, and that's ok. i've got to write it. it's taken so very long to get here. if you should somehow stumble onto my page for whatever reason, you need to know
i forgive you.
– Abbie

The cat skulked back to its home, wounded and prideful and hungry as a lion. It would lick its wounds and get back on the fence again, if it was allowed to roam free. No amount of reason can convince a cat to stick to Tender Vittles in a dish. Even so, a bird has no real reason to be worried. The cat may have claws and guile, but it's also subject to the laws of gravity. The ground is always fast approaching, and birds are blessed with wings.

Joe Keysor, author of *Hitler, the Holocaust, and the Bible*,

is proud to present the 2009

GK Chesterton Award

to

Steve Rzasa

Buffalo, WY

Second Place

(category: 19 and up)

Bio: Steve Rzasa was born and raised in South Jersey, and fell in love with books - especially science fiction novels and historical volumes - at an early age. He earned his bachelor's degree in journalism from Boston University's College of Communications in 2000, and then spent seven years as a reporter and assistant editor at weekly newspapers in Maine. Steve moved to Wyoming in 2007 to become the editor of a weekly newspaper there, and now works at the local library. He and his wife Carrie have two boys and live in Buffalo, Wyoming. His favorite authors include Jeffrey A. Carver, C.J. Cherryh, David Drake, Robert Heinlein, and David Weber. Website: www.steverzasa.com

RESCUED

By Steve Rzasa

Copyright 2009, All Rights Reserved

"Blessed are the merciful, for they shall receive mercy."
Jesus of Nazareth, from the Gospel according to Matthew 5:7

10 AUGUST 2602
LEVESQUE'S STAR SYSTEM

"Target's separating quickly, Skipper."

"I can see that, thanks." Lieutenant Brian Gaudette was floating free in space, feeling relaxed in body but tense in mind. He was actually moving at seven hundred kilometers per second, the same speed as his ship, *Sennebec*. His sapphire blue eyes squinted at the pale gray hull streaming air and metal beneath him. It was increasing its speed every instant, in the wrong direction.

Brian tried to ignore the gleaming surface of the icy world looming beyond the short, stubby interplanetary vessel. Gravity conspired against him, reaching hungrily for its prey.

"Concentrate on keeping clear of debris, RK, and I'll worry about making my date," he muttered into the suit comm.

"You're the Skipper."

On *Sennebec*'s bridge, Ensign RK Palal kept his hands firmly wrapped on the drive controls. The navigation display flashed a red warning at him; he ignored it.

"Shouldn't you attend to that?" Detective Sergeant Eddington Dupre stood well behind him, pasty face pinched with irritation.

"No. Sound's turned off." RK shrugged. "I can tell what she's doing without looking."

"Lovely. Perhaps you can tell her to keep us clear of that moon, using soothing words," Dupre sniped. He deftly plucked a stray hair from his immaculate maroon coat.

RK raised his bushy black eyebrows. "Don't you Kesek guys have anything better to do than bother helmsmen?"

Dupre scowled, and tapped the flat brass badge on his chest. "The purview of the Royal Stability Force is universal."

RK didn't answer. He'd known as soon as he'd seen the name of the target ship why *Koninklijke stabiliteitskracht* – Kesek – had sent a man tagging along on *Sennebec*'s last six rescue patrols.

Pushing the thought aside, he breathed a sigh of relief – Brian's tracking signal on the nav display blinked blue as it merged with the target ship. "He's touched down," RK said. He stabbed the intercom switch above his head. "Lucinda! Ready the cradle. Skipper's aboard and he's gonna bring back the passengers."

"Check. My medics are ready."

Returning his attention to his controls, RK winced. The target ship's velocity was now two kilometers per second faster than his own. He gave *Sennebec* a burst of thrust from its chemical rockets, saving the main drive fuel.

Judging by their distance from the moon's surface, they'd need it.

Brian dragged the space-suited man through the corridor, gritting his teeth as his weight shifted and shoved his arm against a bulkhead. "Skipper!" RK's voice came across the comm in a panic. "We're running out of minutes up here! You wait too long, we won't be climbing out of this gravity well."

"Thanks, RK, I remembered. Sending out the first." He unhooked one of four rescue probes from his suit pack. Slipping the limp man's arms through the probe's straps, he shoved the activation panel. The probe, a simple thruster operated by a homing device, sputtered to life and tugged the man out the hatch into the void. It dragged him across the distance separating the rescue cutter from the damaged ship, to the medics waiting in the *Sennebec*'s cradle – the cavernous hangar bay and rescue hold at its center.

"Lucinda?" Brian called.

"We got him. Nice work, Skipper, the drones couldn't have done it smoother."

"That's why I don't trust 'em." Brian was still moving, this time reaching for the hand of a woman, her dark eyes wide with fear behind her suit's faceplate. He switched comm frequencies. "Ma'am, don't worry. Rescue Corps. You'll be safe in a moment."

The woman nodded sharply, gripping the two tiny boys at her side, both looking faintly comic in their child-sized suits. Brian helped her slide a probe across her back, then showed the boys how to hold on to a second. They rose from the hatch on a flaring plume beside their mother.

"Right. One more?"

"Affirmative, Skipper, eight meters aft of your position," RK said over the comm. "Hurry it up. You got about five minutes."

The ship lurched, sending Brian toward the ceiling. He pushed off with one hand, grimacing. "RK, you are no good for morale aboard my ship. Remind me to put that in your next evaluation."

"If you don't die in a big, hot fireball, you go right ahead, sir."

Brian smirked. He twisted through a corridor, spinning past a collapsed bulkhead, and spotted the last passenger. The teenager was trapped behind a fallen strut.

Switching back to the citizen's band on his suit comm, Brian said, "Stay calm. I'll cut through in a microsec." He drew the plasma torch from his utility pack. Its blue-white blade of flame flared as it started slicing through the metal.

He was almost through when the ship bucked violently. Brian reached for the stanchion but missed. The movement threw him up against the ceiling, slamming him against the surface and knocking the wind out of him. His vision blurred, and sounds went dull.

When he recovered RK was practically screaming. "... Fifty seconds! Skipper, snap out of it! You got less than fifty until the ship's at no return!"

"Quit yelling," Brian groaned. He seized the torch and ripped through the last bit of metal, then put his shoulder to the strut and heaved. The youth, galvanized by the activity, pulled from his side. He managed to slither out in seconds.

"Half a minute!"

"Shut up, RK, that's an order!" Brian grabbed the youth roughly, shouted, "Hold on!" and thrusted with his suit pack down the corridor to the open hatch.

They spiraled out into space, seemingly free, but Brian knew better – and if he hadn't, his omnipresent suit sensors told him the facts. They wouldn't have enough thrust to escape the moon's gravitational pull, even using Brian's suit jets combined with the last probe thruster.

Before he could register fear, Brian saw the silver tube hurtling his way, dragging a cord. "Short rocket, Skipper!" Lucinda called over the comm. "Light it!"

"Outstanding." Brian caught the cord easily, grunting as the projectile yanked on his arm, then affixed it to the magnetic clamps on his suit pack. The rocket was immensely more powerful than the gentler probe thruster. Hesitating, he swiftly made the sign of the cross on his faceplate, then fired off the rocket. The burst of speed kicked him and the youth free of the gravitational pull, but the stress of acceleration proved too much for the boy, who fainted in Brian's grasp. It didn't do him much good, either – he fought off the dark growing at the edges of his vision until he saw Lucinda's space-suited figure reaching for him from a blaze of light.

Then she and the universe spiraled down a drain of stars into blackness.

"You feeling better, Captain?" RK asked.

Brian let Lucinda peel off his white thermal shirt, exposing his chest to the cool sickbay air, as his first officer hovered nearby. Worry etched RK's face with lines – one look at the bruises across Brian's back explained his concern and use of the formal rank.

"Don't get all serious on me. It's nothing a week's worth of leave can't cure," Brian said. He winced as Lucinda injected something into his side. "A little warning next time."

"Yes, sir, Skipper." She ran a med scanner over his chest, brushing past the silver crucifix suspended on a fine chain. Brian grimaced again. "What now?" Lucinda asked.

"Cold. The scanner's cold," Brian complained.

Lucinda grinned, the smile lighting up her warm brown face. "Missed me, did ya?"

"Not particularly. I prefer the galley to sickbay, Chief."

"Now don't blab that in front of my boys. You'll hurt their feelings," Lucinda clucked.

Brian peeked over her shoulder. Two of the ship's medics were assuring the woman Brian had rescued that her husband would heal, while shepherding her and her children from the sickbay. The gangly teenager refused to budge at first, his face drawn and angry, until the mother whispered something and he allowed himself to be led out.

The third medic was frowning over the readouts above one of the sickbay beds. Brian was pleased to see almost all the indicators were green or blue, with just a few yellow – none were dangerous red. A med-robot craned its giraffe-like neck over the injured man's body, scanners playing shimmering light over his serene olive complexion framed by a curly black beard. He was sleeping soundly, courtesy of Lucinda's sedatives, while microscopic nanosurgeons crawled throughout his body, repairing damage.

"He's mending well," the medic called out. "Should be able to wake him and check reflexes in a half hour or so. Got nerve damage though – not something we can fix."

"Thanks, Jimmy," Lucinda said.

Brian returned his attention to his helmsman and first officer. "Where are we off to now?"

"The nearest hospital ship, *HMMC Relief*," RK said. At Brian's questioning look, he added, "Not my fault. Leduc has *Esperanza* laid up at Port Mignery for a main drive overhaul."

"Hmm. *Relief*'ll do. They're not as skilled as Leduc's bunch, but close."

"Well, I'm not picky. We should rendezvous in ten hours. Stefan has the bridge."

"Good."

During the exchange, Detective Sergeant Dupre had entered sickbay. He stood just inside the hatch, eyes narrowed as he took note of every detail. "Who let him in?" Brian muttered, loud enough for the Kesek officer to hear.

Dupre let the comment pass. "That was quite a risk you took, Lieutenant. Doubtless your drones could have done it just as well, without the unnecessary endangerment of your own life," he said smoothly.

Brian bristled at the officer's refusal to call him "Captain," even though Dupre was not a part of the crew and was not required to do so. There were few laws, and fewer traditions, which bound Kesek. "Since our annual operating budget was cut by four percent for two

18

years in a row, I decided to spend what I had on better pay for my people, and on much needed engine maintenance. No fancier drones this year; the ones that broke down stayed broken, and the ones that work can't do the job better than a person anyway," Brian countered. "Don't expect your sympathy, though – your local Kesek office budget increased six and a half percent this year, right?"

"Hardly relevant," Dupre said with a sniff. Turning his attention to Lucinda, he continued, "Chief Wainwright, is the patient fit for interrogation?"

RK's jaw dropped. "Interrogation? Are you nuts?"

Dupre regarded him coolly.

"He'll be talking in a half hour. I figure you already knew that," Lucinda snapped. She applied a patch to a particularly ugly bruise on Brian's left shoulder blade, then stowed her instruments in a drawer. "As for questioning, I won't allow it, not today at least. The man needs a rest."

"That is not possible. His information is vital to solving an ongoing case in the Corazon-Levesque region," Dupre said sternly.

Brian rose, his crucifix sparkling in the bright sickbay lights. Dupre noticed it and scowled. "What kind of information, if you don't mind my asking?" Brian inquired as he pulled his thermal shirt back on. He tapped the white fabric. "Remember? This means I'm the captain."

Lucinda snickered. Dupre shook his head. "It is not your concern, Lieutenant," Dupre said, stressing the rank. "Suffice it to say, it is a matter of a text-in-violation."

That brought a hush over the sickbay. The young medic looked up from his instrument panel. RK muttered something under his breath, balling his fists at his side, but Brian cautioned him with a tiny wave of his little finger. "Why don't you join me in the corridor, Detective Sergeant," Brian said. It was not an invitation.

They ducked through an open hatchway, stepping out into the pale blue-white corridor. RK followed. "Take the bridge, Ensign," Brian said firmly.

RK's jaw muscles worked as he considered Dupre, but he muttered, "Aye, Skipper," and departed.

Brian ran a hand through his close-cropped red hair and sighed deeply. "You mind telling me how you think we're going to recover a text-in-violation when that guy's ship got torn to little pieces over Pembroke's moon?" he asked wearily.

"If it was on the ship, then it is destroyed," Dupre said. "The fact still remains that he willing and knowingly transported that text. He also acquired it from someone. I want to know from whom."

"How do you know he knew?"

"We intercepted his transmissions when he entered this system from Corazon," Dupre said with a smirk. "He thought they were coded, but with Kesek having access to all Marktel communications networks and MarkIntech-manufactured computers, it was a futile hope at best. His message indicated he had the text in hand and was to meet with someone at the sundoor to Giachetto later this week, to hand it off."

Brian frowned. "So you didn't want to hang around the sundoors and wait for him to make the tract shift, afraid he'd spot your own patrol ships."

"Exactly."

Another thought, more sinister, blew coldly across Brian's mind. "Why'd you pick a Rescue Corps cutter?"

Dupre smiled thinly. "We perceived that he might need assistance."

Brian shoved the officer up against the bulkhead, heart suddenly pounding with anger. "You wrecked his ship?"

"Did I say that?" Dupre grabbed Brian's wrists in his own iron grip, and slowly but surely forced the other's hands loose. "I would not go making such accusations of Kesek personnel, Lieutenant, if I were you."

Brian stepped back, putting his hands on his hips, and glared at him. "I won't help you in your witch hunt," he growled.

"You are bound to follow the Charter of Religious Tolerance, and the guidelines of the Convocation on Spiritual Unity, as administered by Kesek," Dupre snapped. "This man's possession of the Koran ..."

"Oh, so now we get particulars!"

" ... Is a blatant and direct violation of that law, which is meant to preserve the stability of the Realm of Five from religious strife," Dupre finished, his voicing rising a notch in volume. "Islam is particularly annoying to Kesek, especially the brand practiced by this man and his ilk, with their insistence on a sole prophet's exclusive revelation from God."

"Maybe your intelligence was wrong."

Dupre shook his head. "The name of his ship is *Abdun Nur*."

"So?"

"It is an Arabic term. It translates roughly as 'follower of the light.'"

"Still not following you."

"In the Muslim tradition, the Koran gives ninety-nine names for

God. An-Nur, or 'the light,' is one of them."

Brian shrugged. "Even so, that Koran has to be burned to crispy atoms by now, if it were a book. They're all illegal, and no one around here's even seen a printer, so what's the problem?"

"The problem, Lieutenant, is that I am not convinced it was a physical copy, but a hidden electronic one, which means that man could still have it."

"And what makes you think you have any right to dictate his beliefs?" Brian countered, jabbing a finger down the corridor toward sickbay.

"Do not think I am blind to your sympathies, Lieutenant." Dupre poked Brian in the chest. "You wear them plainly enough."

"I and my family are members of the Union Synoptic Church," Brian said evenly. "We all have been for years. Monitored and approved by Kesek, isn't it?"

"But your allegiance lies elsewhere, though you hide it well," Dupre hissed. "One would think you are ashamed of your true faith."

Brian clenched his teeth. "I have nothing to be ashamed of," he said, "As God is my witness."

Dupre waggled a finger at him. "Be careful, Lieutenant. Be very careful indeed."

Lucinda was alone in sickbay with the patient when Brian sought them out later. She was puzzling over the readouts from her nanosurgeon control system on her delver. Everyone in the Realm owned one of the handheld devices. They used delvers to access newsgrids on the Reach network, write notes, contact loved ones, file reports, store data, display holograms, play music, and do anything else required. Their society was totally paperless – with the exception of money – thanks to the King's monopoly over information technology.

"Problem, Chief?"

"Oh, hey, Skipper." Lucinda shrugged. "Sort of. The nanosurgeons turned up an implant in this guy, so tiny our initial scans missed it. I didn't remove it – some of those prescription implants release medicine directly into the patient's bloodstream and can pose health hazards if taken out without proper surgical facilities, you know."

"Yeah. So what's the problem?"

"The problem is that his is way too small and isn't leaking any medicine." Lucinda called up an image on her delver, then projected it in a shimmering blue hologram a hand's width from one end of the device. Brian squinted at the hazy image of a cylinder with rounded ends, magnified thousands of times. "You can see the microcircuitry here, and here," Lucinda continued, pointing at two sections.

"Hmm. What is it, then?"

"Dunno. Might be a neuro-enhancer, but it's kind of small. Doesn't make sense to only leave one – you need dozens to provide neural strengthening. Nah, I bet it's a storage device of some kind. Let me get the scanners pinpointed on it, now that I know where it is."

"Okay." Brian rolled his shoulder, working out an ache. "Can you work on it while I talk to this guy?"

Lucinda nodded. "He's conscious, but resting. You can wake him if you like."

Brian straddled the stool beside the bed, planting his hands on the rail. "Sir?"

The man's eyelids fluttered open. He scanned the ceiling, then turned sideways to stare at Brian, anxiety creasing his face. "Where am I?"

"Rescue cutter *HMRC Sennebec*. I'm Captain Brian Gaudette. And you must be ..." Brian drew his own delver and tapped it. "... Abu Saif Zayd al-Faraj, captain and owner of the merchant skipjack *Abdun Nur*, according to your ship's manifest."

"Yes." Zayd frowned. "Where is my family?"

"They're safe. We put them up in a pair of cabins down the corridor."

"My ship. It was damaged. We had a thruster malfunction ..."

"We know." Brian read from the report. "Blew a nice hole in your starboard side, contributing to catastrophic but not immediate decompression. You got your family into their suits and did your best to alter course, but got snagged by the gravity of Pembroke's moon, the nearest body along your trajectory."

"My wife told you this?"

"She did, and so did your oldest boy."

"Saif." Zayd nodded, relaxing. "He was brave. He tried to go back and help our robots with repairs, but he became trapped."

Brian smiled as the memory flashed through him. "Yeah. It took a bit to get him out."

Zayd pushed up with his arms, trying to sit up in bed, but groaned in pain. Brian reached for the bed controls. "Let me."

The bed whined and whirred, easing Zayd into a sitting position. "Thank you," he said. A pause, and then, "My ship is lost?"

"Yes. Our cutter doesn't have the mass or drive capacity to haul a ship of that size out of a gravity well. All we could do was pull you folks off."

"And we are grateful for that. *Ana mamnoon*."

Brian scratched the back of his neck, face reddening. "Yeah. No problem."

"Skipper?" Lucinda gestured from her scanning station. "I'm ready when you are."

"Okay." Brian tensed. "Abu Saif Zayd, we're going to conduct a scan of a foreign object implanted in your body, as allowed under Section Twenty-Two of the Corps' Hazard Regulation Ordinance," he said formally. "Do you wish to file an objection?"

Zayd sighed and closed his eyes. "May I opt out of having the scan?"

"No, sir."

"Then I file no objection."

Brian gave Lucinda a curt nod. She activated the scanner, watching as the slender device descended from the ceiling, its glassy scanning orb rotating into position. It projected a wide, glittering beam across Zayd's body, panning up until it reached his chest. The beam stopped there, focused into a narrow stream of light, and stayed put for half a minute.

A series of beeps drew Brian's attention away from Zayd's rigid face. "Got something?"

Lucinda frowned at the results on her monitor. "Yeah. It's not data storage – the circuitry's a fake."

"Fake?"

"False. Counterfeit. Phony. Bogus. Need more synonyms?"

"Ha, ha."

Lucinda waved her hand at the screen. "Scanner says it's covered with writing. I can project it if you want."

Brian eyed Zayd curiously, but the man continued to stare up at the scanning device. "Go ahead."

Lucinda punched a control, and the blank panel above her scanning equipment lit up. Flowing black script swirled across a golden background. She stared at Zayd, then looked back at the screen. "Empty my fuel tanks," she muttered. "Ion etching. That's an old trick, but the camouflage circuitry makes it harder to detect."

Brian found the curving letters mesmerizing, but he didn't recognize the writing. He came to her side and idly ran a finger across one line. "Can you translate it?" he asked her.

Even as she shook her head in the negative, Zayd began almost whispering, "*Allahu la ilaha illa huwa lahu alasmao alhusna.*"

Brian flinched.

"'Allah! There is no God save Him'," Zayd said, his voice

stronger. "'His are the most beautiful names.' It is verse eight of the twentieth *surah*."

"The Koran," Brian said.

Zayd nodded.

"Blast," Brian spat.

Dupre sat back in his chair, smiling in the shadows of his cramped cabin. It was barely big enough for a bunk, storage bins, and bathroom, and was the furthest accommodations from the bridge. *Sennebec*'s engine noise and vibration made it uncomfortable, but with his headphones firmly in place, Dupre didn't care. He took great pleasure in Zayd's recitation of the *surah*, as delivered to him from sickbay by the listening device Dupre had placed under a stool.

He saved a copy of the recording to his delver, then opened up the warrant file. There were a few blanks left to fill in.

Brian wasn't surprised when the Kesek sergeant turned up on the bridge with an arrest warrant for Zayd. "I expect you to remand him to my custody immediately," Dupre said.

RK snorted. Brian gave him a warning look, then asked, "And where would you like him incarcerated, Detective Sergeant?"

"You have a brig, don't you?"

"No, we don't. This isn't a law enforcement vessel," Brian said. He handed the delver back to Dupre, who snatched it away. "Sickbay should do for now. He's still recovering."

"Very well. He must be placed in restraints, as per Kesek protocol."

"Oh, come on!" RK snapped. "Where's he gonna ..."

"Enough, Ensign." Brian's tone was steely.

RK met his glare with his own disgruntled expression. "Skipper, how can you let this guy ..."

"I said, enough," Brain cut in. "This is Kesek's jurisdiction. Their rules apply. Understood?"

"Yessir." RK hunched over his console, turning his back to them.

Brian rounded on Dupre, catching the smirk growing on his face. "No restraints, Detective Sergeant," Brian stated flatly, and when Dupre protested, he added, "Lucinda and her staff are more than adequate to keep track of him. The guy is not a ship thief or a pirate. We can handle him. You can have him when we dock with *Relief*. Got it?"

"I thought we would continue on to Levesque for transshipment of the prisoner," Dupre said.

"Which part of our rendezvous with a hospital ship did you not understand?" Brian said angrily. "The man is in stable condition, but he needs recovery time in a better facility than I can offer, and I don't want him to wait three days until we get to Levesque."

"The only reason those people were out this far in the system is that they were attempting a clandestine transfer of a text-in-violation." Dupre smiled. "You did an excellent job proving that case."

"Listen to me." Brian brought himself nose to nose with the Kesek man. "You stay the hell away from Zayd and you stay the hell away from his family, or you'll be sorry."

"Interesting choice of words, for a Contritionist traitor."

Brian sucked in a breath.

"Yes, you see I know a great deal about you, Lieutenant," Dupre hissed. "Our budget allows us to employ efficient informants. So do not presume to level threats against me, or there can be great trouble for you. The Corps will not always protect you." He indicated the double golden arrowheads on his collar, the symbols of his rank. "I will interrogate the prisoner as I see fit."

He stalked off the bridge.

That night, alone in his cabin, Brian knelt on the metal grating of the deck. Hands clasped to his chin, face raised to the small, round porthole in his cabin bulkhead, he gazed out at the stars. Making the sign of the cross on his forehead, chest and shoulders, he murmured, "*Au nom du Père, du Fils, et du Saint Espirit, amen.* Lord God, I confess my sins to you and ask your forgiveness. Christ give me strength to do what is right. Show me your will."

He continued on for twenty minutes. By then his knees hurt.

Zayd was talking softly with his wife when Brian came in early the next morning. Lucinda was busily prodding at her patient's ribs, asking every second or third poke if something hurt. Most of Zayd's answers were in the affirmative.

"Mornin', Skipper," Lucinda called.

"You missed breakfast," Brian said with a smile.

"Yeah, well, Jimmy promised to set aside some chow for me. Freeze-dried deliciousness... yum."

Brian snickered.

Zayd nodded in his direction. "Good morning, Captain. Do we need to talk?"

"I think so," Brian said. He handed over his delver. The screen bore Dupre's warrant.

Zayd sighed. His face looked more pale and drawn than the previous day. "I'm sorry to say, the detective sergeant was already here," Zayd said.

Brian shoved the delver into his pocket, turned and kicked a cabinet. Lucinda watched him warily. "Easy on the hardware, Skipper," she cautioned.

Brian rubbed his jaw, saying nothing. "I knew what to expect as soon as I woke up here," Zayd offered. "Shepherding the prophet's writings is a dangerous task in these times."

Brian looked at the slender woman seated by his side. Dressed in flowing, emerald and gold silks draped over a tan shipsuit, her deep, dark eyes watched him carefully. "You endanger your family by doing this," he said.

Zayd looked to his wife, who smiled at him and gripped his hand. "Soraya knew the risk."

"I would not let my children grow up seeing their parents abandon their beliefs to fear," she said softly but firmly.

Brian shook his head. "I can't stop him, you know."

"But you want to," Zayd said.

"Is it that obvious?" Brian dug into the front of his slate gray coveralls. The crucifix dangled between his fingers. "My faith demands I face injustice. Too bad injustice is entrenched in law."

Zayd nodded. "Your kindness will be remembered."

"A lot of good that will do you," Brian grumbled. He dropped the chain, rubbing his face with the heel of his other hand. "Don't take this the wrong way, but I'd rather we'd not found you alive."

"I understand your difficulty," Zayd said, smiling wryly. "A dead body causes fewer problems."

"Yeah. Just sealed up in a bag ..." Brian stopped. A curious look crossed over his face.

"Captain?" Zayd asked. "Are you well?"

Brian didn't answer. He stared off above Zayd's head. Lucinda finally reached across the bed and shook his arm. "Skipper!" she said. "Wake up!"

"Huh? Oh, I'm okay." Brian smiled a small, amused smile. "Just fine."

He walked out of sickbay, reaching for his comm. "RK? Get down to my cabin."

The hospital ship *HMMC Relief* dwarfed the cutter. Two kilometers long, bulbous at the center and tapering to a knife edge at the bow and gaping anti-matter engines at the stern, it cast a shadow over the 120-meter *Sennebec* as RK eased the cutter alongside a row of docking ports.

Dupre stood at the main airlock, rocking back and forth on his heels. He tapped the delver against his free hand, humming a merchantmen's tune he'd picked up on Corazon. This arrest was a fine addition to his record, he was sure.

His smile dimmed a bit when a visibly upset Brian strode toward him, followed by Jimmy pushing a stabilizer capsule on a hoversled. "What is this?" Dupre demanded. "Where is the prisoner?"

Brian rapped the smooth, curved container. "Stasis, thanks to you," he snapped. "You have any idea the stress you caused with your stunt?"

"What are you babbling about?"

"He had a massive and potentially fatal heart attack after you served the warrant. Lucinda – Chief Wainwright barely had time to restart him and get him in the capsule before he died." Brian folded his arms across his chest.

Dupre snorted in disdain. "I trust you have some proof of that."

Brian waved a hand at the capsule.

The readout gave a record of Zayd's body temperature, brain function and heartbeat, among other vital signs. "They look acceptable," Dupre said, squinting.

"Yeah, for someone operating at near death. Chief Wainwright has the nanosurgeons repairing the valve damage his heart suffered, and the capsule won't release him until their work is done. Problem?"

"Not at all. Bring him this way." He pointed a finger beyond Brian. "But make sure his family ..."

"We'll take them back to Levesque, don't worry. Your boys can track them from there."

"Good." Dupre drew himself up into a dignified pose. "Inquiry."

Brian stiffened at the command. But he drew his delver, as instructed. Jimmy scrambled about in his pockets for his own. Dupre produced a black rod from his belt. Its multicolored lights flashed and strobed as the device accessed the contents of both men's delvers, sifting through private communications, data and notes. It raised no alarms.

"Were you hoping for damning evidence?" Brian asked coolly.

"I consider you too clever to put your own spiritual musings down in writing," Dupre said. "Besides, I wanted my own copy of your medic's report on the prisoner's condition – which I just copied. Good day, Lieutenant."

Brian simply nodded.

Jimmy obediently pushed the capsule through the link tube to the *Relief*'s airlock, Dupre in the lead. Captain Thomas Renquist waited for them at the hatch. "Detective Sergeant," he boomed, throaty voice a match to his tall, barrel-chested build. "Welcome."

"Captain. I will maintain a constant watch over this prisoner during his recovery. A Kesek patrol craft is on its way to take us both in two days, you understand."

"Yes, that was all in your commnote," Renquist said.

Dupre smiled. "Excellent." He waved a hand dismissively to Jimmy. "That will be all."

Stabilizer capsules were timed units. They were preset to gradually awaken their occupants and then unseal themselves, unless medical staff sensed a problem in the readouts and overrode the timer. Dupre saw that, according to the medic's report, Zayd's capsule was programmed in concert with the nanosurgeons and would indeed remain sealed until they signaled successful internal repairs.

He was content to wait the four hours, preparing his own reports, giving instructions to the pair of Kesek constables based on *Relief*, and generally basking in the glow of his own satisfaction. But when the time expired, he made sure he was present in the small cubicle of hospital ship's cavernous main sickbay where they'd stored Zayd's capsule.

Captain Renquist joined him. "A momentous capture?"

"Text-in-violation," Dupre said proudly.

"Ah."

The capsule's control panel beeped, its indicators all flashing. A hiss escaped its edges as it unsealed itself and equalized air pressure with the sickbay. A medic reached down and heaved open the lid ...

To reveal a battered rescue drone.

All the color drained from Dupre's face. His delver clattered to the deck, shattering the silence.

Renquist had difficulty smothering his smile. "Oh my. He looks in rough shape."

Dupre rounded on him, nostrils flaring. "Get after them!" he snapped.

"Who?"

"The cutter! Lieutenant Gaudette! You must pursue!"

Renquist shook his head. "I'm afraid you overestimate this ship's capabilities. *Sennebec* can out-accelerate us and cruise circles around my ship any day."

"Then get on the comm and get my patrol ship!" Dupre demanded.

"Sorry, did I forget to mention?" At Dupre's blank look, Renquist put on a fairly poor attempt at a sorrowful expression. "Our comms are down for regular reprogramming. It will be at least two hours. My apologies."

Renquist walked away whistling, as Dupre stared down at the drone and watched his career disappear.

He missed when Renquist's whistle became a murmured song.

"Turn your eyes upon Jesus, look full in his wonderful face ..."

RK chuckled into his hands. "You think it worked?"

Brian grinned. "Thomas was only too willing to assist. Kesek locked his uncle up for proselytizing last year, and his oldest sister disappeared at their hands when he was a boy."

They were in sickbay, sharing canisters of orange spice tea with Zayd and Lucinda. Brian raised a canister in her direction. "Here's to my chief surgeon and her skill with falsifying medical records."

Lucinda clinked canisters with him. "What falsification? Must have been some kind of mistake," she grinned.

"But I still need to go to a hospital, yes?" Zayd asked. "I thought that was necessary."

"Of course, but your injuries aren't nearly as critical as I made them out to be to the dear detective sergeant," Brian explained. "We'll get you to Levesque and get you healed up. I know some people who can help you disappear."

"Your bravery astonishes me, Captain," Zayd said warmly. "In what situation have you placed yourself for my sake?"

"I couldn't let them haul you off," Brian said firmly. "Kesek destroys a little more freedom every time we let them arrest someone for what they believe. We don't need a religious police. Don't worry about me - the Corps looks out for its own."

"Yeah, and it does help that you're something of a local hero on Levesque," RK pointed out.

"True."

Zayd raised an eyebrow as he sipped his tea. Lucinda laughed. "Something of a hero? The man saved the prime minister's boy from a wrecked star-sailer, and is the humble recipient of three Emerald Coil medallions!"

Brian blushed. "C'mon, guys."

Zayd laughed. "Ah, Captain, Allah has put me in great hands, I see. He truly is *As-Salam*, the source of peace and safety, the Most Perfect," he said.

"Zayd, you know all of your Ninety-Nine names for God, don't you?"

"Proudly."

Brian nodded. "Well, there is a name for God that you don't know, and to me, it is the most important."

"And it is ...?"

"Father."

The 2009 Athanatos Online Apologetics Academy

Fyodor Dostoyevsky Award

goes to

J.D. Greening

Port Orchard, WA

Third Place

(Category: 19 and up)

Bio: Pastor Jamie Greening is a preacher who has a passion for communicating the Word of God to today's culture. He uses a variety of styles including story telling, word pictures and literature. He has served First Baptist Church as Senior Pastor since 1999.

Pastor Jamie has a Bachelor of Arts in History from the University of Texas and a Masters of Divinity from Southwestern Seminary. He has also earned a Doctor of Ministry from Beeson Divinity at Samford University.

Jamie and his wife, Kim, have two lovely daughters, Chelsea and Phoebe.

Website: www.fbcpo.org

CONVOCATION

By J. D. Greening

All worshipers of images are put to shame,
who make their boast in worthless idols;
worship him, all you gods!—Psalm 97:7

The meeting place smelled of sweet smoke. An aroma of cedar and myrrh was strong, but pleasant. It was noticeable enough to get the nose's attention but not so strong that it elicited a cough or throat clearing. The scent wafted high through to the top of the large chamber.

The room was lit from above with dazzling torches mounted on large Doric columns. At the top of each column was an impressive golden capital covered with elegant engravings of plants and vines, lilies and flowers. There was no roof. It was open aired. A row of six titanic columns equidistant apart lined each side of the room framing it in a perfect square. Fifteen feet behind the columns lay a stone wall that stretched immeasurably upward beyond the columns. These walls seemed to elevate for miles. The full moon hung overhead with Venus nearby marking the night sky.

In the middle of the room was a large stone altar made from rugged rock. This stone had never been chiseled by hands. The five craftsmen who formed it were named Time, Wind, Rain, Heat, and Cold. Neither iron tool nor hammer had ever touched this megalith. The top and the sides of the stone altar were stained with blood; human blood.

"This reminds me of Athens, or maybe Thebes," said Zeus—to no one in particular. "Yes. I indeed like the columns and hanging there, why yes it is, hanging in the sky is lovely Aphrodite's namesake. This room is almost perfect. It is worthy of Noble Hector or my strong son Hercules."

"It reminds me more of Memphis!" barked another voice. The voice was irritated and annoyed; like one who was spoiling for a fight, or at least a good argument.

Zeus responded bitterly, "I thought I smelled the foul stench of Egypt. Greetings, Ra."

"Why have you called me here, O Zeus the Indulgent?"

"Me?" said Zeus inquisitively. "I was about to ask you the same thing."

Seconds later two more figures appeared around the stone altar. It was a couple: male and female. Both had coned shaped heads and elongated faces.

"Who are you?" asked Zeus.

"I am Baal, Lord of the Sky. This is my consort Asherah. Now who, pray tell, are you?"

"I am Zeus Almighty, King of Olympus, Son of Kronos and god of the Hellenes." Zeus raised his hands and shot a dazzling array of lightening bolts into the upper reaches of the chamber.

"And I am Ra—Dread Lord of the Under…"

"We know who you are. I could spot your stench anywhere."

Asherah cut him off indignantly.

Within seconds the room became populated with all manner of figures: the many armed Shiva, Marduk, the Buddha, Tao, Thor, Sky-Spirit, the feather serpent Quetzalcoatl, along with many, many others. There were thousands of deities who suddenly appeared. Some were animals like the Native American Wolf or the Hindu Brahma. Some were more personified symbols or images, like the Tao or Humanism. After a brief hubbub they all stopped asking why they were there and, curiously, began to mingle like people would at a cocktail party.

The deities seemed to form in affinity groups. Those from the Mediterranean Basin grouped together, and those from the East stood together, the ancient Celtic and Norse deities from Europe mingled as best warrior gods can in a social context, and the mystical tribal gods from the American continents fused into something of a homogenous group. Allah, however, stood off alone in a corner and fumed while plotting domination. He was searching for a burkha to put over the ancient fertility goddess. This particular goddess is known by many names, the most common one is Isis.

Some were having fun with the event. Zeus was taking bets on exactly how long it would take the Sumerian Moon goddess Ishtar to seduce the chaste Buddha. Others were academically comparing and contrasting aspects of their cult. They discussed such things as requirements for novitiates, priestly adherence, ceremonial actions, and holy texts. It was a grand dialogue of comparative religion at the penultimate place. That was, until the main event began.

Just when everyone was getting comfortable and had forgotten where they were and the mysterious circumstances of their gathering; a light.

A great light shown and filled the chamber.

The light was pure. The light was penetrating. Oden held out his hand and the light made an X-Ray of his digits. In a moment of panic Zeus again shot out lightening bolts from his hands, but these seemed pale and yellow compared to the perfect light. The light started with a glow and slowly built up in intensity. When it reached an unbelievable zenith of photoscopic power a billion decibel choir rang out, seemingly from nowhere but everywhere, "Alleluia!" Then, just as suddenly, the light flashed out.

A man stood in its place. He was standing on the blood stained rock altar. At his appearance all the deities were pushed—not pulled—

pushed by the force of the man's gravity toward the marble floor. The gravitational force of the push flattened them prostrate onto their stomachs with their face down. Proud Ra fought to stay on his knees but he could not resist the intractable pressure pushing him into a fully humiliating position.

The man on the stone altar smiled.

"You may rise," he said to the pantheon.

Shiva popped up and proudly asked, "Who do you think you are?" With the question he pointed all of his flailing hands at the man standing on the stone. To the question, the man replied, "I am." As the word "am" came out of his mouth, again the push from above forced all the deities onto the ground once more.

The one on the bloody altar, the only one left standing, sat down upon the stone. It now no longer looked like a stone altar. It now looked like a throne. In his right hand was an iron rod. In his left hand was a shepherd's crook. His legs and feet were bronze. He wore a simple white tunic.

He lifted his iron rod and regally proclaimed, "You may stand. But no more questions."

They all slowly came to their full height. No one said a word, but many glances were exchanged. The dominant feeling among the convocation was confusion and fear. Never before had these deities been so powerless. A moment or two passed and the seated one began to speak.

"My name is Jesus, The Alpha and the Omega."

The Roman god of war Ares shouted, "How can that be? We killed you on that hillside. I remember it. I was there with my faithful Roman soldiers."

Hades chimed in, "Yeah, I was there too. You died. Why won't you stay dead? You're breaking all the rules." The other deities chimed in with similar affirmations, "I was there when we crucified you. I remember!"

Jesus just smiled. "Obviously you are not as powerful as you thought. I am resurrection and I am life. But now it is time for judgment upon all the gods. Let me begin with the greatest pretender of all, Zeus."

Instantly Zeus was front and center before the throne. He opened his mouth to make an argument, a defense, or even a plea. Yet nothing came out. For the first time in his existence Zeus was silent.

"You are not allowed to speak. You have spoken too much already; o Thundering Zeus of the Hellenes. You are guilty. You are indeed very guilty of being a very bad example. You have reflected all that is evil in people: Power, lust, capricious whims, vengeful spite, and anger. You have no love, only eros. You have no compassion, only pathos. You are a sham. You are a bully. You and the whole pantheon over which you preside are evil."

The chief god of the Hellenes knew it was true. He cringed. There was nothing noble in him. Suddenly and without warning Zeus was moved out and another stood in his place. Actually, it was two others who stood before the altar-throne. The Semitic gods Baal and Asherah of Palestine stood where Zeus had just been.

"Baal, you are not alone in your wickedness. Asherah and her evil poles have done more harm than Zeus could ever hope to. No one really ever believed in him. Yet you, you have time and time again lead the peoples of the Near East away from their journey to true faith. You have lured them in with prosperity and wealth, good harvests and fine climate. None of which, incidentally, you have any power over. The only work you ever did was to lie and take credit for what I created.

"Under every green tree and on every hilltop in Palestine you deceived people, male and female. In this deception you model the old liar, Hasatan, and led my people astray. You have added sexual iniquity, prostitution, and violence to humanity. You stand condemned as did your prize pupil, Jezebel."

Within the next few minutes Jesus moved very quickly through many of the shuddering deities. Ra was deemed demonic and oppressive. The pyramids of Egypt do not celebrate his greatness, but stand as a monument to his own vanity. The eagles of the Native American folk religion were dismissed as being too distance, uncaring, and impersonal. Christ condemned Thor as a cheap imitation of Zeus and with the added guilt of encouraging the heinous terrorism of piracy. Quickly the pace intensified as the God of gods summarily judged one false deity after another.

Then the pace slowed down again as the major world deities came before the stone throne.

"Shiva—I will allow you to represent all of the Hindu gods. You have held billions of people hostages to a caste system which benefits the wealthy and protects the privileged. Have you no shame? Do you not see the potential beauty in releasing people from their cultural shackles? You invent oppression and call it religion. Evil!

"You have added to your evil the belief system of past lives and future incarnations. What nonsensical bilge! Do you not know that man is noble? Each human being—woman, man or child is as unique as the Milky Way or as vast as the depth of the oceans? You and your ilk have missed the mark terribly in your estimation of what exactly comprises humanity."

The Lord moved on.

"Oh Buddha; he who is not a god yet venerated; not divine but the enlightened one. Truly, truly I say unto you, you were not far from authentic revelation. In you I find no violence or greed. But you have likewise missed the concept.

The secret to enlightenment is not within the individual. No amount of reflection or meditation can bring truth. It only brings the hint of truth. True enlightenment emanates from the outside and penetrates the soul. You reversed the order and put humanity as the source of spiritual knowledge. What a terrible usurpation. Yes, you were close but still so far away. In your nearness you did not recognize the distance still to go. Instead you mistook *almost there* as *arrived*. This misjudgment led to arrogance and certainty."

A tear formed in the fat Buddha's eye for he knew the truth.

"The Tao must now be examined. Tao, you reflect the timeless truths which I have placed in the created order. There is indeed a balance in nature. Hot must have cold, day must have night, summer is tempered by winter, male is only complete with female. Humans have a yen for every yang and a yang for every yen. Opposites do attract.

"Nevertheless, you are a fraud for you claim to be the way when there can only be one way. I am. There is nothing in you which bringing the harmony you preach. Description is your only gift."

There was only one more left. All had been exposed as insufficient and deceptive. All had been judged, except one. Jesus, still sitting upon the throne called him by name. "Allah," he shouted. "Come here.

"Your time has come. I saved you for the end. You are more recent than these ancient false religions. As with all the others there are elements of truth in some of your words. There is only one God. Alms are proper. Fasts are good. Hospitality pleases me. Good works are a blessing.

"But you have led the sons of Ishmael astray taking them down the

35

path of violence. For centuries you have conquered with the sword, the machine gun, and the suicide bomber. You use fear as a spiritual tactic. You have oppressed the daughters of Eve. You are guilty of turning human beings into automatons. You have rejected your heritage of learning and science. You are guilty of abusing the human race which I made in my image. Therefore, you are guilty of abusing and therefore blaspheming me."

The truth of what the Lord had said to all of these deities penetrated the hard hearts of all. They knew their place in the cosmos. They were not what they thought they were. They stood before him shamed.

King Jesus began to speak to the group as a whole now. "You are created in the image of man; gods and goddesses he made you in his own likeness. Male and female he made you. From his imagination he formed you; out of his own futile thinking he molded you and gave you substance. You were created by him and he breathed into you his own sexual appetites, violent tendencies, legalism, and desire for undisciplined spirituality without moral absolutes in order to justify his sin."

As these words were spoken each of the deities stood with outstretched arms and said in one voice, repeating over and over again:

> *Holy, holy, holy is the Lord God Almighty,*
> *Who was and is and is to come*
> *Worthy are you, our Lord and God,*
> *To receive glory and honor and power,*
> *For you created all things,*
> *And by your will they existed and were created.*

Now the brilliant light re-appeared and grew in ever more intensity. As it came to a crescendo the repeated spoken words were louder and louder until the blend of sound and light were one unified sensory experience. It was as if they were in the exploding core of a supernova. Then it flashed out and became silent. All the deities slowly dissolved into nothingness. Only Jesus was left.

He sighed deeply, stood up, and said, "Now it is time for judgment to begin with the household of God."

The 2009 Anonymously Sponsored George Macdonald Award Goes to:

James Scott Lee

Sparta, WI

Third Place

(category: 19 and up)

Bio: I was home schooled all the way until college, studying by learning on my own whatever I could learn in textbooks and literature. I attended Hillsdale College from which I recently graduated with a BS in Chemistry. I am now pursuing a Ph. D. in Chemistry at Purdue University. Despite this I have always loved the stories of Chesterton and Lewis. However, as short stories go, I find most enjoyment and affinity for those written by Edgar Allen Poe and Graham Greene.

The Devil Child

By James Scott Lee

Copyright May 2009, All Rights Reserved

Under the grass and the pines, the devil child lay. It wasn't dead, no... it was just waiting: waiting for the right sacrifice. The old woman had spent decades trying to bring it back. It was hers, she had brought it into the world, and on the very night of its birth, its father had taken it out. The man had paid, dearly. Paid in such ways as only the best can, she had seen to that. It had been the work of her long long life, finding the best man, deceiving him, and bringing forth the child of death. And in her moment of triumph, it was all taken away; all but the vicious broodings of an old hag.

She brooded and muttered, cursing all, even now when she had lost her power to call down misfortune on others. There had been a time when with this power, she almost ruled the people of a small town she lived by. Its people would bring her anything she asked for. Some obeyed because they were her disciples, others out of fear; but the result was the same, none dared cross her. She had lived there for nearly a century, taking whatever form was best suited to her ends. At times she was an old hag, at others, a lovely, innocent young girl; but inside, she always was herself, bitter, spiteful, and wicked. And now, deserted by the vile spirits she had once called her servants, and divested of all but a shadow of influence in those around her, she schemed to revive her greatest scheme, which was also her greatest failure. The thought made her old bones shake, and with them, the pines creaked.

****

Harriet Lee was sitting in her front yard, clearing it of those blasted black walnuts. She was a frail old woman, well over eighty years old. And yet, there she sat, picking the walnuts out of her yard.

A voice called to her, "Harriet, come!"

She stood. It was not something one would have expected, knowing Mrs. Lee. It would have been much more like her to tell whoever it was to come to her. She was a strong-willed, hard-headed, stiff-necked old woman, and yet she was gracious. But this time, she stood. She brushed off her simple dress, straightened her hair, and walked toward the speaker. Although she walked slowly, and with every sign of rheumatism, she walked erect and proud. Almost it seemed that her rheumatic limbs were less painful, for she walked, not faster, but with more ease.

The voice spoke again. This time much softer audible only to Harriet, "You must go again. She will try once more, but she has not long. You must go to her."

Tears fell from the old woman's face, she knew that the Lord asked the impossible... well, not the impossible, just the nearly impossible. He had asked it of her before, and it had been hard then, when she was young. But now, she was old, ancient by some reckoning, and she was to fight again. Not the prayer warrior at whose approach demons fled that she had been for the past forty years or so, but a real fighter, someone who sought out their enemy, and destroyed their schemes. Also, this time, the man who had actually stopped the witch-woman would not be there to save her like last time. He had already received his eternal crown, moments after saving her. This time.... She shook herself. She knew that the tempters where already there, now that the direct Spirit was gone. She forced herself to recall the past, accurately, and without either rosy glasses or black ones, but with clear and candid remembrance. She hoped to read her enemy from her last actions, and also remember how bad it had been, and that the Tempter really didn't care what age his victims were, he deluded them all, merely changing his tactics depending on age. Whereas now she felt frail and incapable, last time she had felt strong and ready. Both were deceptions. Ah, she had let her mind wander, back to the past.

Her first intimation that her friend had gone wrong was, as it usually is, a small thing. Chance comments are hard to remember sixty, or even seventy years later. But there it lurked at the fringe of her memory like a ravenous wolf, waiting for the fire to die before he leaps upon his prey. What she could still remember with a certainty was that it was a hot day in the summer: she could see the little stream running by, hear the mill grinding, the mosquitoes all round them, she even remembered her friend killing one on her own face, right as it was full up. Perhaps it was that little bloodstain on her face that made the impression worse. She remembered everything about the incident, except what had actually caused those chills, and goose pimples, and that horrid sick feeling in the bottom of her stomach. Even now, she felt that sickening chill. Tea... Tea would cure the memory of its chill.

As she sipped her tea her thoughts sank back into her ancient memories, to the next event that stuck out in the chronicle of her friends earthly damnation. Her friend had damned herself, slowly shoving further and further away from God, taking as many as she could with her.... But there, she wondered again.

Her mind sank back into its revere, forgetting its need for the tea, which grew cold in her hands. Flitting among a myriad of small things, which took all of them to build into something odd. Not even evil, merely odd when recounted. A look here, a word there, her friend had been very good at concealing how far gone she was. Determining this, she went, in her mind, to the very back corner where she had stored her worst memories. She didn't want to bring them back to her consciousness, but that evil chill coming from the little girl with a bloodstain on her cheek must be stopped. Wickedness loved it when people forgot how evil it was, so she would remember and stop her friend once more.

She went to the worst memory of all, one which would not make much sense to anyone else without a little background. It was the spring of her twentieth year when it all the little things became a big thing. All the minute hints resolved into one huge catastrophe. She had had to stop it. She was chosen, not by fate or chance, but by the Lord. She hadn't done so well last time, she had only partially stopped the witch-woman, Hedy. She had rebelled from her calling, and the town suffered. She hadn't really been the one to stop the witch last time anyway. But he was gone. He had been willing to die for his child, and she... she had stood there in the light of those burning bones, in that small cluster of onlookers, knowing that something must be done, but petrified by fear. The man, who had so loved his child, and his wife, even though she was a witch, and his child who was cursed.... His death had been terrible, and she had stood there knowing that that should have been her action. He had charged into the flames and carried his doubly accursed wife, and his dieing child out of the flames. The flames had consumed him, for they were not ordinary flames. They were the very fires of hell, and he had endured them to save the evil witch-woman. Hers had been that place, and looking back, those doubts and indecisions that stopped her then now were revealed to be what they were: fear, and the devil. Her love for her friend had not been enough to even try to save her from her evil deed.

The witch was unscarred, but the man had died with his child. They should have been buried together, the man's ashes to protect the child's ashes, to keep the witch-woman's bony hands away. But that is not what happened; nothing had gone right. She still had the child's body, and the evils she had planned were not stopped, they were merely delayed. This time, the witch was old, hardened, and practiced. It is a rule with witches that they become more powerful as their bodies weaken. They dominate more of the lesser spirits, and befriend more of the greater ones. This time, it would not be so simple. Just snatching her out of her fiery magic circle wouldn't do, it would not be possible for anyone now; especially not an old, weak, woman like herself. Stopping her supply of offerings wouldn't work either. Everyone in the town was either her eager slave, was conquered by abject fear, or hadn't the slightest inkling about what was really going on. No, the food, powders, potions, and sacrifices would flow to her house until either the Devil came to claim his own, or Christ did. Either way, the witch would be damned. And they had been friends. There only remained confrontation.

She shook herself, stood up, put on her coat, and left the house. It was a long walk, but it was impossible to get the witch-woman's real house any other way. It was true that her real house and the one everybody else saw were in the same place, and looked almost the same. The differences were subtle. But one couldn't see the witch for what she really was, unless one walked the whole distance, with the purpose of seeing the witch. The house everyone else saw was just an illusion, carefully maintained over many, many years. The only place that was the same place in both the illusion and the reality was the little grave where she had cunningly buried her little child. That place was a small little gravestone, overgrown with weeds under a willow tree, in both places.

As she walked she was assailed with the same doubts and fears as last time she had made this walk. This time, she ignored them. They were whispers and images put into her mind from elsewhere, and as such had no bearing on her present task. She arrived, and the house saw her.

"So you came," the house said, "My mistress said you might. She also said not to worry too much about it, you will fail this time too. You are an insignificant wobbling chunk of senile flesh! What do you plan to do before one who commands the gods themselves?"

"I did not come to talk to a house. Where is your mistress?"

"Inside."

"Let me in, I have business with her."

"What if I say... No!"

"It's alright, let her in."

The thin creaking voice had come from inside the sentient house, but it was not the house that spoke. The voice made one think of dried pine needles. Not the pleasant warm afternoon smell, but their shriveledness, their brittle point, their deadness. It was wispy like the sound of the wind blowing through stands of dead pines, whose needles clung to them still, in a hopeless mockery of life.

The house lowered itself. Harriet whispered a prayer, crossed herself, and entered. Her palms itched badly.

****

No one after could understand the fire that night. It raged all night, it burned with such a delight of burning as must have inspired the ancients to believe there were spirits in the fire. Everything burned, orange strove with blue, and white with black as the fire raged over the countryside, white hot, burning everything in its path. Its path was not like a normal fire, this fire had chosen what it would burn, and avoided what desired not to burn. The swamp burned and the winds blew it everywhere, yet when it reached the town, only some places were burnt. Where there had been two pubs, one was burned and the other untouched; where there had been two churches, one was ashes and the other whole; the halving of the town did not extend to the dwelling places of the inhabitants. No, most of the houses were burnt down: those burnt were wholly burnt; those untouched wholly untouched. The firemen were ineffective; the fires burned insatiably and then went out like they began, together.

The strangest occurrence found in this strange incident was in the ashes of a house just out of town. There, two corpses of very old women were found; one burnt down the bones, and the other untouched by the flames.

41

Athanatos Christian Ministries

is proud to present the 2009

Leo Tolstoy Award

to

Joseph A. Raborg

Hazlet, NJ

Third Place

(Category: 19 and up)

Bio: Joseph Anthony Raborg was born in New York City. Shortly thereafter, his family relocated to Hazlet New Jersey, and the author was fortunate in having two more siblings: a younger brother, Thomas, entered the world in 1988 and a younger sister in 1996. Having a shy and studious disposition, Joseph devoted himself to reading books and remembers the children's books St. Jerome and the Lion, St. George and the Dragon, and an adaptation of the tales concerning Erik the Red as his particular favorites. Under the encouragement of his parents, he transferred his energy from children's and comic books (then, Garfield and Calvin and Hobbes; now, he still reads comics, but these are exclusively of Japanese extraction) to a wide range of subjects spanning the natural, literary, historical, and religious areas of study. In high school, he discovered that he had a knack for language and is now capable of reading works written in Latin, Greek, Japanese, and French. One day, he hopes to expand his linguistic talents since translators take far too many liberties in his opinion.

It seems only natural that this bookworm wishes to write a book of his own. He has been writing a fantasy fiction novel long before he turned his pen to "The Death of St. Magnus of Orkney" and hopes to finish the revisions within a year-if he can stop finding new ways to distract himself.

The Death of St. Magnus of Orkney
Based on the Account in the Orkneyinga Saga

By Joseph A. Raborg

Copyright 2009, All Rights Reserved

May this miserable sinner receive aid from his glorious subject, the holy Earl Magnus, for the glory of the Refuge of Sinners and Oak of the Saints, who never refuses the repentant, constantly knocks at the hearts of those lost in sin, and empowers men to perform such magnanimous deeds.

A dragon ship sails the northernmost end of the North Sea, bearing Earl Hakon Paulsson, the proud ruler of half of Orkney. His ship bristles with coruscating spears and bright shields adorn its sides. Here and there, a man rows upon the still sea from his bench, draped in a dull, grey hauberk. Almost none of the men aboard lack a helm and secondary weapon. The crew exercised their duties with peculiar vigor, eager to reach their destination.

Yet, this martial preparedness fills one man, Havard Gunnason, with terrible apprehension; but, he reminds himself that earls and princes oft wish to exhibit their might, and this need not bode ill for the meeting which would seal the peace between the two earls. Earl Hakon himself had arranged this meeting after level-headed men interceded for the two opposing armies and averted civil war. Each earl would bring a single ship to the meeting in order to seal the peace.

But Havard marveled that so few of the leading men within Hakon's earldom represented themselves onboard his ship. The crew consisted mainly of Hakon's own retainers and guests, including two which Havard did not only feel the mission would be better off without, but the entire world besides: the two brothers, Sigurd and Sighvat. Havard glared at the two of them as they murmured filthy lies into Earl Hakon's ears. Before these two began filling Hakon's head with thoughts of fame and exciting the earl's already rapacious ambition, the two earls ruled Orkney with hearts amicable and benevolent towards one another—as befits cousins. Now, no doubt, the two again were trying to incite civil war.

Havard stepped forward to prevent the two worm-tongued advisors from turning Hakon's heart. "Earl Hakon, this is beautiful weather we were fortuned to have. If only the wind was a little stronger. It bodes well for the restoration of peace to these islands—as it was before."

Sigurd turned his pock-marked face toward this new speaker. "Yes, before that greedy Earl begged our king to let him have a share of his patrimony. He's only useful for starting up trouble, I tell you!"

Sighvat added his own opinion: "Orkney is two small for two earls. Hakon was ruling well enough before Magnus decided King of Scots' hospitality wasn't good enough for him."

"Now, I won't have you slandering Earl Magnus before his cousin, our esteemed lord," Havard countered. "And it seems to me they held a wonderful joint rule—with justice lacking for none—until quite recently."

Here the earl himself thought best to intervene. "Havard is right. We did jointly rule Orkney in a splendid fashion. Everyone had nothing but praise for us; perhaps for my cousin most of all."

"Not at all, earl! We citizens of your domain—I speak the unanimous opinion—would not trade you for Magnus or anyone else."

"Nonsense," Sighvat said. "People are all greedy. The only reason people flock to Magnus is because he throws gold and silver right and left. It's a wonder that anyone is still poor."

"Yes," Sigurd agreed. "I don't care a fig about those who extol Magnus's piety. He just knows that liberal princes gain more friends." Sigurd added the following with a significant look in Havard's direction. "I've heard that he's given especially great gifts to chieftains from Earl Hakon's domain."

The hue of Havard's reddening face approached the darkness of his brown beard. "Earl Hakon, I think these two are merely jealous of you for possessing so saintly a cousin. Some say he's remained so chaste that he has not even consummated his marriage."

This comment caused the other three to guffaw.

The earl said: "I do believe that you've mistaken my brother for a certain Englishman."

Havard smiled. "Or St. Joseph. Without peer save for Our Lady, who surpasses all the saints."

"Blessed be Mary, the Holy Mother of God," Hakon said with his two sycophants struggling to catch up.

"Dragon ships off the port side!" shouted the lookout in the bow of the vessel.

Sure enough, seven ships rounded a point of land and began to approach Hakon's vessel. Their emergence took Havard aback. Each one glimmered with spear points and their blazing red and yellow shields reflected the sun's radiance.

Havard turned to the earl. "Earl, whose ships are these? Ought we prepare for the worst?"

"No, no, my good Havard, they're mine."

Havard paled. "But your agreement stipulated only one ship."

"Don't worry yourself. I merely intend to restore peace to these islands, and showing superior force will ensure us of coming ahead at the meeting."

"Why, Havard," said Sigurd. "Don't you agree with his lordship's plan?"

"I can guarantee you, Earl Hakon, that Earl Magnus will not come with more than one—"

"Of course," Sighvat said. "I don't know about his saintliness, but the man is rather simple-minded."

"Now, men," Hakon said. "I'll not have you say any more about my good cousin."

Havard said: "Well, my lord, please permit me to take my leave for the moment."

The earl granted it. Havard walked to the shield rimmed railing and looked out upon the advancing fleet. Changing his line of sight, he examined the calm, blue sea as a gentle zephyr refreshed him. He sighed.

"I would have been a wonderful day to return peace to Orkney. God keep Magnus!"

When everyone ceased paying attention to him, he slipped overboard and swam to a deserted island.

On the same cerulean and serene sea, Earl Magnus in his lone vessel set their course for Egilsay. Onboard, Magnus had collected all the peace-loving men of his earldom, who had contributed much to preventing the outbreak of battle between the two earls. According to their means, each man possessed a sword or ax, but spears stood absent from the decks and shields from the sides. Not a man, not even Magnus himself, thought to wear a hauberk. Magnus, wearing an azure woolen tunic and green linen pants clasped with a golden buckled leather belt, sat against the mainmast, watching the blue sky with even bluer eyes. The breeze hardly disturbed his golden locks as it brushed across his fine, intelligent countenance.

The gentle weather necessitated that rowers propel the ship along. Two of whom, Svein and Holdbodi, palavered over the eccentricities of their blessed earl and good friend. Not a few times did someone chuckle, while the other made sly remarks concerning their lord's mental state.

"See him? Our good earl?" Svein began. "He's staring blankly at the sky again."

"Well, it is a beautiful sky to gander at," Holdbodi replied. "And very few on this boat have the leisure to do that."

"You know what they say about men who do that?"

"What, Svein?"

"They either enter a monastery or burn down a barn."

After both laughed, Holdbodi said: "Well, that makes our earl a future arsonist. They don't make monks out of married men."

"What marriage? I tell you, my wife would beat me if I permitted the flower of her maidenhood to bloom so long."

"Well, they're strange people: the earl and his wife. But, I've never seen a happier couple."

"I wish all rulers would be so strange, then there would be paradise on earth."

"One can't have a double paradise, you know."

"Who says? I think that your association with our strange earl is turning your brain."

"Well, may he rule long and continue to bless us with this prosperity."

"Hmm...I wonder what the chances are of that."

"What do you mean, you depressing bastard?"

"The fellow's too honest. I told him he should bring twenty ships—not one—to this meeting."

"But the agreement—"

"You think Hakon's going to keep his word? I'm sure he's eager to fulfill that heathen soothsayer's prophecy about him and his descendents ruling all Orkney."

"Ha, ha, ha! Well, Magnus is young yet, but that time will come eventually—even if it is only Hakon's descendents." Holdbodi grinned. "You know, this Hakon should have learned from a Norwegian king of the same name. He rules well enough, but his ambition makes him detestable. If he rids himself of that, he might well merit the cognomen 'good.'"

"Why, yes! I'll even make a song for this Hakon entering Valhalla and greeting Odin—along with all the other devils in hell. That son of a—"

Neither modesty nor human voice interrupted Svein, but a towering wave rose from the mirror-flat sea and crashed upon Earl Magnus's meditative form. All the crew yanked their oars back in the boat and rushed to surround Magnus, who now stood brushing the excess water from his tunic with a placid demeanor. The other questioned Magnus and themselves what this meant, marveling that such a wave could spring from so board-like a sea.

Magnus turned to his men. "I think that your worries are quite justified: it looks like that prophecy about cousin Hakon will come true."

Some, ignorant of the rumor, said: "What do you mean, my lord?"

"This wave foretells my death. We may have to be open to the idea that cousin Hakon may not be exactly honest with us."

"Then let's turn back!" Holdbodi exclaimed. "Raise some men, and defeat that treacherous earl!"

The rest shouted their agreement. Magnus raised his hand for silence.

"No, I have no evidence that he shall betray us. I hope to the Lord that it is not so! Onward! Let me only keep my word and everything happen as God wills!"

"But, Earl Magnus—"

Magnus interrupted his housecarl with a smile. "I thank you for being concerned Holdbodi and for the mutual affection we've always shared. Nevertheless, *Deus vult!*"

This silenced all further protest, and the mournful ship continued its course to that glorious isle, fortuned to be soon nourished with the blood of a saint!

After several hours, Magnus and his companions at last reached their goal, the undulating island of Egilsay. Though a small farm might support itself here and there, much of the soil consisted of moss covered, black rocks. This feature predominated the area where they landed: the inhabitants saw nothing better to do with the land than build a small church there. As the sun now began to fall in the saffron sky of the west, Magnus called his companions together and sent two so that the parish priest might prepare himself for hearing confessions and performing Mass.

"Whether I live or die, I wish to meet my cousin with a clean heart."

All his men declared that they would fight to the death for Magnus's sake. Magnus ordered them to do otherwise: "No, I would not have you fight to save my life—if Hakon really values ruling Orkney at the price of kinslaughter…We shall see. In any event, let there be peace in Orkney, and let the will of God be fulfilled."

They all knew that the earl stood beyond persuasion and prayed that the earl's premonition of his death turned out false. Hakon and his men needed a longer time to arrive and would not present themselves until the morning. So, they formed a line for confession, and, once the Sacrament of Reconciliation cleansed one and all, they took their seats in Church to carry out divine worship.

The walls of the church bore several statues of saints both ancient and modern until the end wall; where a tabernacle was located to the left of the altar and its great cross, while the right displayed a statue of the Holy Family. Interspersed with the statues of the saints, stained glass windows described the life of the Church's patron, St. Paul, from the stoning of St. Stephen until his own death at Rome.

The earl sat in the front pew, leaning forward as if to gain a deeper understanding of the divine mysteries by placing his head on its very bosom. The leading men of his domain all prayed that evil be averted from Magnus, while Magnus prayed that he might act according to the honorable tradition of his ancestors and the friends of God. As soon as Mass ended, Magnus announced that he would continue to stay within the Church, but that they may find shelter among the inhabitants or return to their ship. The majority took Magnus up on his offer so that they might discuss what they ought to do should Earl Hakon turn hostile toward them. But several, such as Holdbodi and Svein, remained praying with Magnus.

Holdbodi hoped that he might be given the opportunity to dissuade Magnus from this baneful course of action. Holdbodi edged nearer to the pew where Magnus prayed using his rosary of wooden beads and bided his time as he awaited Magnus to finish. However, Magnus's companions dropped off to sleep one by one long ere Magnus finished. Leaden sleep at last pressed shut even Holdbodi's green eyes and loyal mind.

Then, Magnus himself became weary at his prayers and, crossing himself and putting away his rosary, he rose to look at his companions, hoping that there might be one with whom he could unburden his anxieties. Yet, scanning the whole Church, he found not a man that fleshly necessity had spared. Indeed, sleep even began to swirl his thoughts.

"Ah, you fool," he told himself. "Why do you expect comfort from men? But this church feels so warm. I should like to spend my final night, what I so greatly fear to be my final night, sending as many prayers to the Savior as I may."

With these words, he left St. Paul's for the cool evening breezes.

Outside the church, a full moon illumined the island, though not a single light from any building save those in the church augmented the natural light of the night sky. A million millions of stars greeted Magnus's sight: not one constellation seemed absent. Grief invaded

Magnus's thoughts considering that he might never see them again. Magnus stepped through the mossy rocks until he found a hillside with great rocks shielding his view of the church, but not its victory-promising steeple. Turning about in this salient, Magnus fancied that from here he could fend off a substantial force of men. He shook the thought aside.

Kneeling toward the shining, black sea, he renewed his prayers. Yet, thoughts of his kingdom and how much he would forsake through his death began to assail him. Try as he might, the sting of losing all his possessions and the splendid world itself distracted him from prayer until shame wrung tears from his eyes.

"O Lord! I am so unworthy of Thee that the thought of losing all my possessions and created joys causes me real distress. Send Thy grace to this unworthy servant so that my heart may be free of them. Hail Mary…"

Thus he beseeched Our Lord, Our Lady, and those saints dearest to him. Soon, his tears dried and gentle resignation calmed his anxiety. In the midst of this peace, the cacophony of a fatigued man struggling in the tide startled Magnus, who rushed to help the naufrague onto the pebbly strand. Magnus turned the man on his side so that he might cough out the water from his lungs.

"Oh!" He coughed out some water. "That hurts!"

"Havard!" Magnus exclaimed. "How have you come here in this state? I thought you would be travelling with cousin Hakon."

"Oh…" Havard coughed several more times for good measure. "I beg your pardon, earl. I have many things to tell you. Earl Hakon intends your death."

"I know…I know, Havard."

"Then what are you still doing here? My lord, you must leave Egilsay at once and prepare for war."

"No, there shall be peace. If cousin Hakon really desires my life, he can have it; though, I hope to dissuade him from the awful sin of kinslaughter."

"That man is too ambitious." Havard rose from his side to a sitting position. "He will only content himself by your death."

"What do I have to fear from death? Our Lord—"

"But think of your possessions! This glorious world! Who has returned from the dead? Who has told us what it is like?"

"Havard, I never knew you to advise me like a pagan."

But Magnus could not hide the tremble in his voice as anxieties he thought quelled returned with renewed vigor. He saw a sly smile flash across Havard's face and knew not what to make of it. His interlocutor pressed the question.

"You boast of the greatest wealth in Orkney: such fine clothing, beautiful weapons, a great manor, the choicest food and drink. Earl Hakon covets all these things—"

"Oh, truly? If my cousin was in such want, he need only have told me."

"It would not do any good: the world itself would not satisfy the man. So, fight for your rightful possessions. The man does not deserve the scrawniest fowl on your estate."

Magnus became silent for a while, as Havard said many more things. Reviling the greed of Hakon, yet saying how Magnus ought to enjoy his property. He described the very wonderful things of the world which Magnus, as a young man, might look forward to enjoy for many years. While his advisor noticed not the shifting attention of the young man, Magnus's eyes strayed to the cross of the church steeple. At last, Magnus obtained his answer.

"But I myself do not deserve the scrawniest fowl on my estate." With Havard taken aback by this remark, Magnus continued: "All these things came to me through the will of God. Why should I boast of things I have received? We know that a greater estate awaits the faithful with Our Father in Heaven."

"Oh, that can wait. You are yet a young man. Many years still ahead of you."

"But why trade eternity for a few more years of exile? Who would be so absurd as to believe heaven less wonderful and joyful than earth?" A divine spark flickered in Magnus's eyes, and sweet consolation welled up in his heart. "Praise be to Our Lord—"

"Wait! Hear me out!"

"—Jesus Christ!"

Havard, the image of that man—which Magnus mistook for the man himself—vanished before Magnus's eyes. But not before he saw the demon's eyes fill with animosity and anguish, and his mouth form an unspeakable curse. With his knees shaking, fear took hold of Magnus. He bowed down and crossed himself.

"These are the enemies with whom I contend? Oh, aid me, O Lord! This one attempted to dissuade me from honoring my oath to cousin Hakon through greed and trusting in created things. But I was saved by Thy Holy Name." Here he prayed the Act of Faith. "In thanksgiving for this precious deliverance, I shall offer to go on a pilgrimage to Rome—nay, even to Mt. Calvary itself—and never return to Orkney should my cousin spare me."

Delighted with his new-found resolution, Magnus offered further thanks to God until footsteps disturbed his prayer. Seeking his new companion, he discovered Svein coming toward him.

"Your lordship, when I awoke, I saw that you were gone and went to look for you." Turning to the sea, he said: "Only on the night of a full moon does the sea seem so brilliant."

"Indeed."

"Please pardon me, Earl Magnus, but I and the others can't agree to what you're doing: sacrificing yourself for the sake of your infernal cousin, Earl Hakon."

Here Magnus chuckled. "Oh, cousin Hakon is really getting the short end of the deal: I shall wend to eternal life with God, while he'll be stuck managing Orkney."

Svein's countenance became morose: "I wonder how many souls perished thinking the same thought, only to find themselves in hell."

This remark rent the core of Magnus's being in pieces. So much so, that he fell backward on the ground. Ignoring Svein's entreaties as to his physical condition, Magnus said: "What an awful thing to say…Is not confidence in one's salvation one of the gifts often given to those about to die?"

"Maybe, but think of those monks who beg for a few more moments so that they may have a longer time to repent before the end. And we laymen don't hold a candle to them."

"Those poor holy men who do penance for us sinners as well as themselves!"

"Good luck to them: sin is as common as dirt. The best remedy is a long life with many chances to repent."

Magnus smiled. "A long life is not necessarily a good one. It is fortunate that the Church provides the sacraments of Penance and the Eucharist. Between the two, all sins are crushed."

"I don't know. Perhaps I sinned four times between Reconciliation and Communion and sixteen between then and now."

Magnus knit his brows. "That strikes me as remarkably irresponsible, Svein—even if you were the most hardened of sinners."

To Magnus's astonishment, Svein guffawed for several moments—needing to hold onto his sides lest he begin rolling on the floor—before he regained his sullen countenance. "I suppose that I was exaggerating a bit. Still, you would agree that dying now isn't the best thing."

The rosary in Magnus's chest pocket rustled, reminding him of its presence. He clasped it and gazed upon the final scene of his dear Lord's mission. Then, looking at Svein, he said: "Why would Our Lord, who sacrificed so much for us, be so eager to damn us and set venial sins against our entry into the Kingdom? From sin He has freed us. Through His strength none ever need turn their backs on Him."

"But think of how many sins we daily commit—"

"I expect to be punished for these, but not eternally. His purifying fire shall save me from the punishing flames of hell. As long as I do not turn my back on Him in my last moments, He shall fight for me and save me."

"Oh really? I can number the sins against you since you gained the use of reason until this very day, and they exceed the very stars!"

Magnus thrust forth his crucifix. "St. Michael smite thee back to the depths of hell to remain there for a thousand years, demon!"

Like the first, this one too vanished. Ire coursed through Magnus's stout heart. "I see how they work, these foul creatures! Against beginners, they use material things to lure them from the spiritual. Against the more advanced, they tempt them to despair. Well, I shall fight and fight against them even after this body perishes. That is the essential thing: never quitting no matter how many times or how deeply one falls." Here he knelt and recited the Act of Hope. Then he said: "I shall make a second offer should cousin Hakon turn down the first: that I might be sent into a dungeon and held under guard by our friends in Scotland for the rest of my days; for the light of God inspires even those locked away in the deepest pits."

The need for rest dunned his weary eyes. No longer did Magnus deem it necessary to keep his vigil. He stood up to return to his men in the church and did not progress far before he saw Svein and Holdbodi searching for him. He hailed the two men to approach him.

Holdbodi spoke first: "There you are, Earl Magnus! I hoped that I might be permitted to speak with you."

"Blessed be the name of Jesus Christ."

At once, they responded in unison: "Both now and forever."

A smile lit Magnus's visage. "How happy I am to see friendly faces! Speak your mind, Holdbodi."

The earl and the other two sat down after the earl beckoned them to do so. Once they were seated, Holdbodi began: "My lord, please don't do this thing. Don't permit Hakon to kill you. You have brought real justice to Orkney and succor to the poor. Where would we be without you, dear friend?"

Magnus held back the tears which threatened to burst from his eyes and stifled the affection and joy welling from his very viscera. Suffering from so great an emotion, Magnus could not reply.

"There was never a better earl than you or a better friend. I daresay, there was never a better husband. How your poor wife will miss you! It's wrong! It's unjust for you to sacrifice your life for Hakon's ambition!"

"Oh...my dear friends...my dear wife..."

"Please escape with us. Dawn has not yet broken. Free us from the unlawful tyranny Hakon threatens us with!"

Magnus placed a hand on Holdbodi's shoulder. "Cousin Hakon is a splendid ruler, Holdbodi. I know you'll miss me, but he shall not bring tyranny."

"Still, you can't leave your family and friends like this. It's wrong!"

The sun just began to rise and illuminate Magnus's mournful features. "You're right in a way, Holdbodi. But there is a higher justice only fulfilled through charity: all souls belong to God. Through the perversity of their own hearts, many men are lost. It is a great shame to lose even one, and God does not receive his proper due: the love of all men. My death shall not destroy your souls, but may even save my cousin and many others besides."

"But dying for Hakon..."

"Love your enemies. I have dispensed enough justice; enough criminals have been incarcerated through my judgment. That is not very great: it is not so wonderful that souls are sent to hell through God's justice, but that so many are saved through his mercy. *Deus caritas est.* And I pray that my poor efforts may reveal the love of God to the poor sinners of this world. Even if cousin Hakon kills me, I shall not cease praying for his soul before the very face of God."

Svein announced: "There are Hakon's men! They're searching the church! It is too late."

Indeed, as he spoke, a formidable company of armored men with spears and shields entered St. Paul's Church to search for the blessed earl.

Holdbodi mourned: "So true. We no longer have a chance to escape. It seems like the greater shame to me that so great a man will lose his life to the likes of Hakon."

Magnus sighed. "If the vilest murderer had been given the same graces I have so often neglected, people might imagine that Christ himself had returned. But I hope to at least end my life for the glory of God." Here he spoke the Act of Charity along with his tearing men. After they finished, he said: "Don't fear. I have one last offer to deter my cousin from kinslaughter—this he will accept: that he mutilates me however he wishes or blinds me and casts me in a dungeon."

This remark caused renewed wails from these two most loyal vassals. St. Magnus now comforted his two companions and bade them pray to God for courage and for the sake of all poor sinners.

After some time, Hakon's men satisfied themselves that the earl had not hidden himself in the church and came back outside. Magnus rose to the top of a hill and summoned them, telling them not to bother seeking him elsewhere. The soldiers looked askance at one another, but they shrugged and began to approach. All of Magnus's other men saw that they were at a disadvantage of eight to one and had already surrendered to Hakon's men, in obedience to Magnus's command.

As Magnus and his two companions awaited the soldiers' arrival, Svein said: "Well, it was a great honor to have had you as our earl."

Holdbodi still had tears in his eyes which he desired to wipe away ere Hakon's men arrived. "Yes, if you can, continue to rule Orkney from paradise."

Magnus laughed. "Indeed, I might just rule Orkney as a king; in the country where all are kings and queens, and where the lowliest handmaid has risen to become the greatest empress."

"That is precisely what I shall tell, Earl Hakon: you're his king now."

"No, no, no. Don't use me to vex my dear cousin. He may yet be saved. Obey this as my final command."

Both his companions replied: "As you wish, my lord."

"Now, let us say a few prayers."

Thus it happened that Hakon's men came upon Magnus and his friends praying. Though they clashed their spears against their shields and hollered so that the citizens of London might hear them, Magnus and his men did not glance up from their prayers until they had finished. The men never saw another soul face certain death so calmly.

When Hakon arrived at this place along with Sigurd, Sighvat and the rest of his chieftains, Magnus crossed himself and greeted his cousin, who returned this greeting with the news that he must die.

Magnus replied: "Kinsman, you ought not to have broken your oath, though evil advisors probably led you to the deed. But, I would not have you sin further by killing an innocent man and a kinsman; so I will offer you three alternatives."

Sigurd, Sighvat, and the chieftains demanded to know what Magnus had to say. Magnus described his first proposal and Hakon's men turned it down. They refused the second proposal more vehemently than the first. During this time, Hakon glanced from his men to the holy figure of his cousin saint Magnus and wondered what he should do.

At last, Magnus described his final offer: "Well, cousin Hakon, God knows I'm perfectly willing to lose my life if I might save your soul. So, I shall make this last offer: mutilate me however you wish or, having blinded me, cast me into a dungeon rather than murdering me."

Before the leading men of his district could reply for him, Hakon shouted: "I accept! Without any other conditions!"

Yet, his men rose up against him and said: "We're tired of conflicts between the two earls and civil wars rising every few years! It's either him or you!"

"But what can he do while blind and imprisoned?"

"We'll have either your life or his! One of the earls must die!"

Flustered, Hakon responded: "Well, let Magnus die. I am yet young and enjoy ruling people and places."

A broad smile covered Magnus's face and he knelt down to shed tears before God. Hakon no longer stood as a full murderer! He had argued with his men and fought for Magnus's life! Only when pressed by the fear of death did he break at last.

Hakon told Ofeig, his standard bearer, to execute the deed, but Ofeig said: "Earl Hakon, I've played my part in this business as far as I'm going to go. Find another headsman!"

Rebuffed with such strength, Hakon did not ask again, but turned to scan the rest of his men. All showed forth a stony countenance save Lifolf, his cook, who, as he fought back tears, stood marveling at the great saint.

"Lifolf! Come here. You shall perform the deed!"

Instead of complying, Lifolf could no longer hold back his tears and wept aloud. Magnus noticed his fellow sufferer and went up to comfort him. Slapping him on the shoulder, he said: "Don't weep! Such a deed can bring only fame to the one who accomplishes it. Show your bravery and my clothes are yours according to old customs." Here Magnus took off his tunic and dried Lifolf's eyes. "The man who gave you this order has far more guilt than you." He turned to address his cousin: "Cousin, please permit me to say some final prayers."

Hakon shouted his agreement before any of his men could put forward a different idea. Having received his permission, Magnus prayed for both his friends and murderers, wishing prosperity for the former and forgiveness for the latter. He also prayed that the last of his sins may be blotted out upon the spilling of his blood so that he might be greeted by the hosts of heaven.

Once he was finished, he was led away to the place of execution. On the way there, he turned one more time to speak with Lifolf.

"Kill me by striking with all your strength upon my skull. I have not committed a crime, and so do not deserve to be killed like a thief." Remembrance of the deed remaining for him renewed the tears in Lifolf's eyes. "Do not fear. I have prayed that you obtain the mercy of God. On your last day, I hope to see you again in paradise."

Once they reached the place of execution, Magnus knelt and crossed himself to receive the blow. Hakon had been feeling sick during the entire episode and forced himself to watch his cousin's death with clenched teeth. Lifolf took one last look at Hakon to confirm his lord's will. Hakon gave a brief nod. Lifolf then raised his ax and struck Magnus's death blow.

Sensing the mood, Sigurd and Sighvat had remained quiet for a long time. But a spirit of rashness, deriving from being long ignored, rose up in Sigurd.

"Good! He got what he deserved. All hail Hakon as the earl of all Orkney!" Hakon endured the cheers with a stoic countenance. Sigurd continued: "Let the body of this greedy man, Magnus, lie here for the crows to peck at!"

Sigurd crossed the wrong line. Hakon drew his sword and smote Sigurd's helm with such a blow from the pommel that Sigurd lay stunned upon the ground. Then the earl landed several blows into the man's stomach with his hard boots. Blood leaked from the corners of his mouth.

"Why isn't it you lying dead out there instead of that godly man? Leave him for the crows! No! My cousin shall be given a funeral before God and men as he would have wished." He turned to Sighvat. "Sighvat! You and your brother are never to return to Orkney as long as I live. I give you one week to gather your things and depart."

As the years lengthened, the people of Orkney saw that though Earl Magnus perished, he continued to help them from his throne in God's kingdom. Earl Hakon never committed such a grave sin ever again and died beloved of his people. Those sick and insane went to St. Magnus's tomb and were healed. To this very day, a cathedral marks the victorious death of St. Magnus and God's victory over the devil as revealed in this friend of God. Glory be to the Father, and to the Son, and to the Holy Spirit, as it was in the beginning, is now, and ever shall be, world without end. Amen.

The Confident Christianity 2009

John Wycliffe Award

for an author writing in English as a second language

Goes to

Adel Emmanuel

Cairo, Egypt

(Category: 19 and up)

Bio: I am a fresh graduate pharmacist. I graduated from Ahin Shams University in Cairo. I was greatly encouraged by my friends to write some stories and participate in some writing competitions and contests; they saw something good in my words.

I participated in a competition had been held this winter 2009 in college with my one-page very short story. I have won the first place. As a result, I was more encouraged to participate in international contests, like ACM writing contest, and it seemed that God, as well as Debbie Thompson, also saw something good in my words.

I like to read very much to the contemporary novelists like Paulo Coelho, his masterpiece The Alchemist had touched me so much and had given me faith, will and hope. and I really adore classical writers like Tolstoy and his marvelous War and Peace.

Oracle of the Wicked Land is my very first short story.

The Oracle Of The Wicked Land

By Adel Emmanuel

Copyright 2009, All Rights Reserved

On a sunny morning, Adam looked to the sky and smiled, "Good morning, God". Then a sweet breeze of air played with his ears with the voice of God, "Good morning, Adam"

Walking among the green trees, Adam saw lions playing with

rabbits, hawks flying with doves, crocodiles drinking with zebras. All lived with each other in peace, harmony, and were enjoying together the magnificent natural world that God had created for them all.

This was how animals lived in the garden that God had made, The Garden of Eden.

Adam was the head of all creatures the LORD God had made. He was the most powerful creature of God, the man of God.

He went in a search for his helper that God had made for him, Eve. Although the garden was full of animals and the expanse of the sky full of birds, Adam found his joy with Eve. He loved the whole garden, but with Eve, it was different. She was part of him. He could talk with all the animals, but without Eve, he was so lonely.

When God wanted to create a man, he created Adam. Imagine how charming Adam was. When God wanted to create a woman, he created Eve. Imagine how beautiful Eve was. They were head over heels in love. A love story just as God wanted it to be. Love for them was a life style. They simply worked in the garden, ate from its fruits and loved each other.

One day, Adam went searching for Eve. He found her standing before a very beautiful tree talking with a serpent. He came closer so that he could hear what they were talking about.

The serpent was craftier than any of the wild animals the LORD God had made. They were talking about the tree, the tree of knowledge of good and evil.

The woman said to the serpent, "We may eat fruit from the trees in the garden, but God did say, 'You must not eat fruit from the tree that is in the middle of the garden, or you will die.' "

"You will not surely die," the serpent said to Eve, "for God knows that when you eat of it your eyes will be opened, and you will be like God, knowing good and evil."

When she saw that the fruit of the tree was good for food and pleasing to the eye, and also desirable for gaining wisdom, she took some. Then suddenly Adam interfered and took the fruit from her hand and threw it to the ground, "Do not eat," Adam shouted angrily, "the LORD God has commanded, 'we must not eat of the tree that is in the middle of the garden'. Do not listen to the serpent!"

The serpent then fled from Adam and Eve's faces.

Eve felt happy that Adam arrived in time. "The tree was really beautiful," she said.

Adam took her hand and showed her every other tree in the Garden. "They are all beautiful, Eve"

Adam lay with his wife, and she conceived and Cain was the first fruit of their love. Later she gave birth to his brother Abel.

Cain, who had a strong body, was cultivating the garden. He

loved the trees, the flowers and any plant having roots in the ground. Unlike Cain, Abel, who was leaner than Cain, loved the animals. He was a shepherd.

One day, when Cain was working with the plants, he met with the serpent, "You are much stronger even than Adam." the serpent said, "You can rule over Adam, Eve, Abel and the others."

Cain stopped working, sighed, "And why do I need something like that?" Cain asked.

The serpent said, "Because you deserve it. Do you know what this tree is, Cain?"

Cain looked to the beautiful tree, "Yes, it is the forbidden tree from which I must not eat or I will die"

The serpent laughed loudly, "No one dies, Cain. He, who eats from this tree, will rule over the world, be like the LORD God himself. What does such a strong man like you need, except power, authority and omnipotence?"

Cain did not think for a long time. He was the strongest. He should rule over the world like God, the mighty. He took some fruit from the tree and ate. Then his eyes were opened and he realized he was naked; He hid among the trees, so that no one could see him.

Evil entered his soul. Knowledge of evil was enough to spoil the beautiful nature of humanity. Cain's mind then was opened to know what God did not like him to know.

In the cool of the day, the LORD God was walking in the garden as usual, when he called Cain, "Cain, where are you?"

"I heard you in the garden, and I was afraid because I was naked; so I hid." Cain replied.

"Who told you that you were naked? Have you eaten from the tree that I commanded you not to eat from?"

"The serpent deceived me, and I ate." Cain replied in shame.

So the LORD God said to Cain "Because you have listened to the serpent, you are expelled from the garden"

Cain then was filled with ignominy. He silently walked out of the Garden wearing animal skin garments made by God.

The LORD God said, "Cain has now become like one of us, knowing good and evil. He must not be allowed to reach out his hand and take also from the tree of life and eat, and live forever." So the LORD God placed around the Garden of Eden cherubim and a flaming sword flashing back and forth to guard the way to the tree of life.

Through the silence of the night, Cain wandered in the land outside of the garden feeling very sad and lonely.

There was darkness everywhere. As he got deeper into the land he heard a woman sobbing. He walked towards her voice. There was a woman dressed in blue sitting on a big rounded rock in front of a big tree. When he got closer the woman lifted her head and looked at him. She was white like ice, with long dark black hair and a small pointed nose. Her eyes were black with no eyeballs.

Cain looked at her and said, "Who are you? I thought that people lived only in the garden the LORD God made."

"You thought wrong," she replied. "God created me even before earth and heaven."

"Before Earth!" Cain wondered in his mind.

After a short pause, he went on,"Why were you crying?" he asked.

"Because this is where tears exist. Out of Eden, you should get used of crying, fear, pain, despair, dissatisfaction, grief, not getting what is desired, separation from those you loved and association with the unbeloved."

Cain sat on the ground beside her. He seemed confused with her words. He didn't understand what she meant. "What do you mean?" he asked.

"Forget about Eden. The days of Eden are gone. Now, they are imprisoned in the garrison of your memory and will be no more, Cain."

He was astonished that she knew his name.

The woman sensed how he felt and knew what went on in his mind. She continued, "I was waiting for you. I am the one who called you from Eden."

Her answer filled his mind with curiosity and doubt, he asked, "How did you call me from Eden?"

"I am the soul of the serpent. I have talked to you through his tongue."

Cain dreaded the woman. He let out a shudder and asked, "Who are you?"

The woman then walked away giving her back to him, hid behind the tree and vanished. Cain walked behind her and whirled around the tree, when a serpent, which was hanging on a branch of the tree, looked at him and hissed loudly. There were many of them hanging on all branches. Cain got mad and said to the serpent, "You deceived me." The serpent fell on the ground and bit his heel. It was the first time that Cain experienced pain, which was very hard on him. Ten minutes later, he experienced another new thing, which was even harder: fever. His temperature rose rapidly, and his vision blurred, then he fainted on the ground.

In the Garden of Eden, three days later, everyone was talking about Cain, how he fell into the serpent's trap. For Eve, it was different; even though she had many sons and daughters, she mourned Cain's loss. He was the eldest son, the dearest.

From the moment Cain was driven out the Garden, she kept asking herself, "Why? Why did God permit this to happen? Did he not know that Cain would eat the fruit since he knows everything? Why did he even create this tree? Did He want us to eat it in the first place, if so, then why did he create us? And why did he let the serpent do what he wanted to do?"

She went to Adam for the tenth time asking him her eternal questions. But finally Adam had an answer, "God created us because he loved us even before he created us from the dust. He knew us in his mind and loved us. He created the garden for us to live happily forever with him. And about the serpent and the tree, they are one and of one origin, one purpose, evil exists. God's love does not oppose his truthfulness and integrity. He respected us, and wanted to let us know that from the moment that good existed, evil existed. And we have to choose one to follow and to live within. God chose good for us. So, we should not choose evil for ourselves"

Eve glanced at Adam and let her tears fall. "I wish I was the one who had eaten from that tree. I wish you had not prevented me. Then, I would be with my son now. Bring me my son back, Adam. I do not care if he sinned, I just want him back."

Adam felt the same grief not less than hers. He mourned him too inside his heart. He knew it was impossible to bring him back as he had disobeyed God's command, "What can I do, Eve? Even God has stopped walking in the garden as he used to since he drove Cain out of it. But I will ask him for I know he will listen to my voice in prayers. Surely he will."

On the next day, Adam raised his heart to God and prayed, "Bless me my LORD for I want to talk to you. I know that you are angry and sad for Cain has disobeyed your command. I am not praying for the wicked land, but for Cain, for he is yours. I am not in the wicked land, but he is. Holy God, protect him by the power of your name. I want Cain to be with me wherever I am. We feel no joy in Eden, not anymore, while Cain is alone in the wicked land under your eternal damnation. Eve and I are begging your endless mercies. We want Cain back. And you, the mighty God of the universe, certainly can find a way. Bless me my LORD and I will not be blamed."

Cain opened one eye, then the other. He was lying on a woody bed in an empty rocky hut. He stood on his feet exploring where he was, when a short, bald, old man with a long black beard entered the hut, "Well, our man woke up. How are you now, Cain?" asked the short man.

Cain wondered that there were many of people outside of the garden. "Fine, Sir. But who are you?"

The short man laughed, "You ask a lot of questions, Cain. Anyway, I am Belial."

Cain did not have a clue who Belial was. "Where am I, Belial?" Cain asked again.

"You are in the city of Babel, the biggest city of the wicked land. After you were bit by the serpent, we got you here in order to heal you. Are we not kind?" Belial replied.

"Thank you, Belial. Of course you are very kind"

After sleeping for three days, Cain discovered another new sensation. "I am hungry."

Belial laughed again, "Go outside and help yourself." Cain went outside the hut. There were many strange people working with some strange instruments like they were preparing for something. He looked at the trees, they were blooming. He went to one of them, but it was an unfruitful. Going to one after another, he found all were unfruitful. He went back to Belial, "All the trees are unfruitful, Sir. How can I eat from them?"

Belial seemed happy with Cain's confusion, "Yes, they are. You must work the land; through painful toil you will eat of it all the days of your life. Are we not kind?" Cain was not amused by Belial's words this time.

Belial glanced at Cain with a roguish look, "You have to choose between three choices: the first, till the arid land and eat from your own work, the second, die of hunger."

Cain asked him about the third option and Belial smiled and answered, "We serve and feed you."

Cain did not hesitate; he chose the third option. "But there is nothing for free," Belial said.

"What do you want?"

Belial seemed happier as if he had achieved his desire, "that is something Lucifer will tell you about."

"But who is Lucifer?" Cain asked him.

"Oh, that one you met three days before; the oracle of the wicked land."

Michael was the archangel of the cherubim guarding the Garden, leader of the army of angels. He was the right hand of God the LORD.

God had made winds his angels, flames of fire his servants, so that they could serve him and his creatures. Their will was God's. God's will was keeping his children well protected and safe. Although he could have his will done without any angel, he loved to share his work with his discreet creatures humans as well as angels.

Eve went to Michael asking about Adam. She had searched for him everywhere for days but could not find him. She was overwhelmed by bitterness and sorrow of missing Cain and now of not finding Adam.

She asked him if it was still possible that Cain might return back to Eden. "Look, Eve. It is one sky and one God over the Garden of Eden and over the wicked land. And you should know that what is impossible with men is possible with God." Then he ordered her to go back into the garden but gave her no answer about Adam. She went back wondering where Adam could be.

Belial went with Cain to meet Lucifer. On their way, he kept telling Cain about her, "Lucifer is the greatest creature of God. Her crown and jewels are set and mounted in gold. She was the most powerful archangel. She was on the holy mount of God, walked among the fiery stones. She shook the earth, made kingdoms tremble. She made the world a desert and overthrew its cities."

Cain was amazed at how powerful she was. He felt it when he was talking to her before. He felt a kind of energy spreading through the air into his body possessing his mind, heart and sensations. "And then what happened? She does not look like an angel." Cain asked.

"Being the most powerful archangel was not an easy task. The more difficult the task is, the more glory you should possess. But God despised her. Instead of the glory she deserved, he gave her a curse."

They arrived to the desired place. It was a very huge, black castle on the top of a hill. There was a dark cloud over it, through which lightening hit but did not harm the castle.

They entered through a big woody door that was opened with the help of two black giant beasts.

When Cain entered the wide hall of the castle, there were five chairs. The one in the middle was the biggest, it was Lucifer's. The other four were alike. On three of them, there were three men sitting. The farthest one on the left was empty. Belial went and sat on the empty chair leaving Cain standing before the most powerful five figures in the wicked land, the chancery of evil.

Lucifer introduced the four men to Cain, "The farthest one on the right is Beelzebub - who was black skinny small man with two bony wings - the lord of bats. Next to him is Sataniel - who was a giant like an elephant with two big pointed ears and a dragon tail - lord of wild beasts. The one on my left is Iblis - who was hairy like a monkey with a head of a wolf - lord of evil weapons. And the one on the far left, whom I am sure that you know him already, is Belial, the lord of the wicked humans. And I am Lucifer, the fallen cherub, the morning star, the queen of the four devils and the oracle of the wicked land. I have all the wisdom, knowledge and power that neither angel nor archangel has."

Cain could hardly keep himself from falling on the ground. He realized his lowliness in front of those lords of evil. That was exactly what Lucifer wanted him to feel.

"Now, Cain" she said. "Belial has told me that you have chosen the third option; being fed by us. Is that true?"

"Yes, it is."

"Well, here, in the wicked land, nothing is for free. You must obey our commands."

"I will, my Queen," Cain replied while giving her a low bow.

Lucifer glanced at Belial with a little smile on her face and then looked back to Cain and continued, "Well, God has despoiled my glory. He despised me as if I were made of dust. He glorified the dust-made humans and scorned me, the light-made star. But I have saved my power. And I want my glory back."

"How will you do that?" Cain asked.

"Only by eating from the tree of life, can I return to my former glory and be like God, the mighty."

"So, what has that to do with me?" Cain asked.

"You are my battle, Cain. Your blood is my power. Your damnation is my solution."

"I do not get the point!" Cain said with growing fear.

Belial lost his head. He stood on his feet and said to Cain, "We have to drink from your blood in order to win our battle against Michael and his hosts. Your blood will give us the glory God has given you, and we will be back to our first state, the strongest host of angels."

Hearing these words, Cain stared at Belial. He tried to run out of the castle but he wasn't feeling his feet anymore. He stood still for a while confused and astonished. At last he said "You lied to me, Belial. I should not have trusted you."

Then Lucifer interrupted him, "Cain, now you have just two options: agree or die. Take your time thinking. Time is my ally"

Outside the castle, all the devils gathered around the Death Lake, they called it the Abyss. There were hundreds of flying bats, hundreds of wild beasts and hundreds of smoky chariots that were drawn by reddish black horses. They were beating the drums with their woody sticks. It was like a kind of festival.

Lucifer left the castle with the other four devils and Cain.

When the crowd saw the Oracle, they all kneeled down. Belial took Cain and threw him into the Abyss which was shallow and salty. With two ropes, Belial tied Cain's both hands to two wooden posts, one post at one side of the Lake, the other at the opposite side. He tied one hand to each post. Cain's hands were stretched painfully. He was hardly able to breathe.

Belial cut Cain's two wrist arteries so that his blood could fall in the Lake and been mingled with its dark water.

Lucifer stood at the bank of the Lake and was the first to drink from its water.

When she drank, she had transformed into a white giant lion having giant eagle's wings. She hit the air with her wings and flew over the Abyss.

After her, all the devils drank from the water, but no one transformed, they only became more powerful.

Cain, after being the strongest of men, was a bony skeleton dressed by human skin. He was so weakened. He cried, "May the day of my birth perish, and the night it was said 'a boy is born', may that night be barren, may not shouts of joy be heard in it. Why is life given to a man whose way is hidden. I have no peace, no quietness; I have no rest, but only turmoil."

Sataniel asked Lucifer, "Now, we have drunk from human blood. How can we defeat Michael? We are not stronger than him, and he also has a very strong army"

"I have a plan," Lucifer replied.

Michael was walking amidst his army like every other day when he felt an earthquake shake the biggest mountains of the earth. He lifted his head to the sky and saw hundreds of bats flying blocking the rays of the rising sun. Then hundreds of running beasts with smoky chariots on the ground, from the misty mountain appeared to his sight led by the flying white lion, Lucifer.

Michael raised his flaming sword to the sky, and shouted, "Defend the garden of the LORD."

Michael fought strongly, as did his army. They divided into three parts; one fighting the flying bats; one fighting the ground beasts; the last one standing behind, defending the Garden and the people within.

They fought each other all day. No one could see if the sun was still in the sky or not, for it was darkness at noon because of the flying bats and the clouds of dust made by the ground beasts. But they knew that the day was wearing away.

Michael and his angels were still powerful and strong while the devils were exhausted and weakened.

Beelzebub and Sataniel ordered their hosts to retreat. They went back to Babel, while Michael and the angels rejoiced because they won their battle against the devils.

In Babel, Cain was tied by the ropes to the posts. He was so hungry. There were some pigs being fed beside the Abyss. He longed to fill his stomach with the pods that the pigs were eating, but none gave him anything. He was filled with disgrace.

He remembered when he was young in Eden. He was a five-year-old boy playing with his favorite friend the eagle, or Chogan as Cain used to call him. When the five-year old boy just thought to eat, Chogan flew to the sky and reached up to the tallest tree in the garden bringing back to Cain a very beautiful fruit.

Cain sighed remembering these times in Eden. "Chogan, I am so very hungry." Cain told himself, "I long to see you, my brothers, my sisters and my parents again." Then he thought of what Lucifer had told him the first time they met, 'separation from the loved and association with the unbeloved.' She was right.

At this moment, he saw that the devils were back the same as they had gone. He knew that they must have been defeated. He was happy at first. But when he heard Beelzebub and Sataniel telling Belial, who did not go with them, the sneaky plan of the battle, he became sad and despaired.

Lucifer, after she had drunk from Cain's blood, was strong enough to beat all the angels, but not Michael.

But she had a plan.

She could transform herself to any shape, to any creature, even to an angel of light. When they waged the war against the angels, she had transformed herself to an angel. She walked through the fighting armies without any angel to notice her presence. And now she succeeded in her plan.

Lucifer entered the Garden, searching for the tree of life, but she found nothing. She was confused. She knew where the tree should be, but it was not there. She transformed herself back to the giant lion and scared all the people. She fought against the third host of angels, those were guarding people, and won. She gathered all the people in the middle of the garden, and prevented their escape.

When Michael came back from the battle, he was astonished by the turn of events. He tried to fight the lion, but he stopped and got back when Lucifer told him to do so or she would kill all the people.

"You were blameless in your ways from the day you were created till the wickedness was found in you. You were filled with violence, and you sinned. Your heart became proud on account of your beauty, and you corrupted your wisdom because of your splendor. You have come to a horrible end and will be no more." Michael said to Lucifer.

Lucifer laughed so loudly that all the people closed their ears with their fingers. "I drank from Cain's blood, and I will eat from the tree of life and get my glory back. You are the one who will come to a horrible end, Michael, for I will destroy you, I will reduce you to ashes. And now tell me, where is the tree of life? Or I will kill all the people."

"God the LORD hid it. None, except him, knows where it is."

"Well, I will take all those people with me as hostages. And I will keep them forever till your LORD changes his mind. Or till you do so."

Lucifer then took all people, except for Adam because no one knew where he was, and flew through the sky on her way back to Babel.

Taking people as hostages deserved a celebration party in Babel, especially when they were naked people. Naked people meant that they were virtuous people. And devils adore virtuous people; their suffering, their pain and their despair.

During the celebration, they drank all the night from their favorite wine, the bloody water of the Abyss.

One of the devils asked Belial if they could drink from the blood of the naked people. "Shut up, you idiot. We can not drink from the blood of naked people. If we did, we are all dead forever. We are only allowed to drink from sinned-humans' blood, like Cain's, to gain more power. We can bother naked people, scare them, but we can cause no harm to them. Their blood will burn us forever."

While they were celebrating, Cain looked up at the sky praying to God. He cried tears of joy when he saw an eagle flying over the Abyss. It was Chogan. Cain considered this a good omen, "I knew that there was still hope."

The devils celebrated all evening till they were exhausted. It was a long day for them; a spiritual battle at noon, and dancing celebrations in the evening.

The next morning, Lucifer ordered Belial to bring all the naked people to the Abyss. He did so.

When Eve saw Cain was tied by the ropes, she cried and grieved over him.

"Eve, I know that you know where the tree of life is. You better tell me where it is or I will kill Cain, your dearest son, in front of your eyes now."

Eve fell to the ground and cried, "I do not know where the tree is. I beg your pardon, leave my son alone."

"You beg my pardon!" Lucifer said in derision. "What pardon?" Then she ordered Iblis to bring their strongest weapon, the curved sword of envy and ordered him to slay Cain.

Eve ran towards Cain when Iblis got the sword but Beelzebub stopped her. She wept and wailed but no one listened.

Iblis hit Cain on his head preparing him to be slain, when Cain shouted, "My God, my God, why have you forsaken me?" Then Iblis slew Cain.

After few days, Lucifer decided to go searching again for the hidden tree. She ordered all the devils to drink from the lake,where Cain's dead body laid, preparing for the probable war. All the devils obeyed the order and together drank from the bloody lake.

Suddenly, there was light shining in the bottom of the lake. The light gathered at one point on Cain's body. Cain arose, returned to life. All the devils, including Lucifer, stared at him. He was a dead body a moment ago. How could he come back to life like that?

Then all the devils, who drank from the lake, were burnt to ashes.

No one could believe that all at once the devils existed no more. When Cain unwound the ropes and got out the Abyss, people recognized him, for he was not Cain, he was Adam, an innocent man.

Lucifer was the only who did not drink from the blood of Adam, so she lived. Adam, now much stronger than she, forced Lucifer to run away, roaming through the earth.

After Lucifer had gone, Cain appeared from behind the trees. He went and drank from the lake, and was transformed into a virtuous man by the power of Adam's blood.

All the people asked Adam how he came back to life. He replied, "After I had prayed to God the LORD, he took me to the tree which he had moved onto Horeb, the mountain of God, in the form of a burning bush. Though the bush was on fire it did not burn up. He ordered me to eat.

I ate and was transformed into the most powerful man in the universe. I can do everything. I can give my soul and bring it back to me whenever I like. I went to Cain after the festival of the devils had finished, wore the garments that he was wearing, unwound him and tied myself instead of him."

Eve was the happiest. All the people congratulated her and Cain. During their way back to Eden, Adam opened his mouth and said, "Cain, if you thought that you were the only who was suffering in the wicked land, you were wrong. We suffered with you, even God the mighty. All of us went through your struggle by soul. Your pain was our pain. Your tear was our tear. Even if you had sinned, you were still one of us and will be forever, we love you wherever you have been. And as for God, he did not drive you out the garden, your sin did. Your sanctity did not bring you back to Eden, his love did. He has just done his miracle, bringing you back to your first state through me.

From now on, be self-controlled and alert. Your enemy, Lucifer, prowls around like a roaring lion looking for someone to devour. Resist her, standing firm in the faith, because you know that your brothers throughout the world are undergoing the same kind of sufferings."

Cain hugged Adam with tears in his eyes, with happiness in his heart. He looked towards the people, his family, and said at last, "Surely my father took up my infirmities and carried my sorrows. He was pierced for my transgression, he was crushed for iniquity; the punishment that brought me peace was upon him, and by his wounds I am healed. The LORD God had sent his man to me. Surely God is my salvation; I will trust and not be afraid. The LORD, the LORD, is my strength and my song; he has become my salvation."

"3Then Jesus told them this parable: 4"Suppose one of you has a hundred sheep and loses one of them. Does he not leave the ninety-nine in the open country and go after the lost sheep until he finds it?"(Luke 15: 3-4)

The Athanatos Christian Ministries 2009

JRR Tolkien Award

goes to

Elizabeth Chance

Warner Robins, GA

First Place

(Category: High School)

Bio: Elizabeth Chance lives in Warner Robins, Georgia, with her parents, her sister, Rebecca, and their two dogs. She and her sister were homeschooled until high school when they entered Wynfield Christian Academy. Elizabeth graduated this year from Wynfield.

Elizabeth has enjoyed writing and acting ever since her best friend Hannah introduced her to these hobbies over eight years ago. She hopes one day to publish more of her writing.

Azrael

Elizabeth Chance

Copyright 2009, All Rights Reserved

Black water, as still and as quiet as death. The water stretched out over the otherwise-empty expanse as smooth and innocuous-appearing as a plate of glass. But jagged rocks and other, more sinister, things lurked underneath the surface, just waiting for some unfortunate ship to run up on them.

A thousand derelicts lay impaled under the blackness, lulled by the false hope of land which was, in reality, deadly obsidian. Many were the ships that had sailed toward the rocks, naively sailing to their deaths. No true land in sight, no one to hear their dying cries, no one to help.

The bleak, frigid water with its hidden dangers cried out: desolate; desolate.

X 3000 B.C. X

Crack! Metal met flesh. A rivulet of blood ran down the slave's back. "Faster, dogs!" the overseer ordered, a growl in his voice. The slaves obeyed quickly, fear propelling their tired bodies.

On the first level of the boat, Prince Nen stood, staring intently into the blackness. The sound of the oars plunging into the dark sea discomfited him. "By the gods," he murmured, fingering his ankh, "I should have never sailed against Nut's wishes." A pang of fear, something foreign to the great Prince, swept through Nen's body as the boat plunged on through the dark and deathly silent water.

"My Prince," Sef interrupted fearfully, bowing low at Prince Nen's feet. "Rise and speak," Nen barked, his austere gaze showing a bit of fatigue and a lot of anxiety.

"The slaves are uprising!" Sef finally spoke, shifting his eyes about the deck nervously, "They say Isis and Nenet were not appeased by our sacrifices on the isle of Nerine, from whence we departed; they do not wish to continue the journey and risk angering them."

The Prince drew himself up, sweat glistening on his well-toned body. Uncertain of what to do, he adjusted his golden headdress proudly; it glinted only dully in the crushing darkness, but it was respected nonetheless. The cool touch of the hammered gold infused him with courage, allowing him to speak with confidence. "I am the son of Pharaoh," he snapped haughtily, "And I shall remind them of that. My father is the morning and evening star; he *is* Egypt! The power of Egypt lies with him as granted by the gods and goddesses; the deities always agree with him, and with me. We sacrificed two times our normal offerings, and the deities *were* appeased."

Nen turned away from Sef and lifted his head to the sky. Surely Isis, his own personal goddess, would not let anything happen to him! Why, he was practically a god himself. . . . Still, Isis could be very unpredictable at times, and it would hurt nothing to please her and Nenet even more.

"Sef, bring the pyres and a white bull," Nen decided, "I shall comfort the slaves and ensure a smoother voyage."

A relieved smile on his face, Sef bowed once more, and hurried off to the ship's storehouse. But just as he reached the storehouse, the boat ground to a halt, slamming him into the wall.

Pain shot through his neck and head, his body collapsing to the deck. "By the gods!" he muttered angrily, staring out into the black expanse.

At first the sea remained silent. Sef pushed himself to his feet, holding onto the side of the boat. The throbbing ache was beginning to ebb in his neck, and he shuffled toward the door.

A faint moaning sound caught his attention, and he froze. A blue streak of electricity arched out of the water, striking his chest. It hissed and crackled as it swarmed over his whole body in milliseconds. Sef let out a yell of pain before collapsing to the deck again, this time dead.

The whole boat began to shake as a guttural roar split the silence. Splinters of wood sheared off of the sides of the boat, plummeting to the waves below. Suddenly the boat imploded and shattered, raining debris over a large area. Water churned everywhere, throwing the crew into a mass panic.

The thrashings and vociferous yells of one hundred doomed souls echoed over the wasteland of water for but a few moments before they were silenced one-by-one.

The black ocean slowly calmed down as the last bits of wood sank into its depths.

'Another one claimed without a fight,' the cause of the desolation thought, slowly sinking down into the black oblivion along with the shards of the devoured ships. The darkness began to absorb its body as it smiled to itself, 'Once again I prevail.' It rested the mass of its body on the bottom and closed its eyes, the frigid water slowly lulling Death to sleep.

X 2000 B.C. X

"Reprehensible Hebrews," Abiah muttered, gripping the side of the ship in anger, "We will destroy them." He glared across the dark water at his fleet.

Four of the massive war vessels were filled with stallions of royal birth and the finest chariots; seven contained the very best of Canaan's warriors; and his own ship . . . on it he carried ten prophets of the supreme Baal.

It also carried Havivah, the elect priestess of said god. A smile crossed Abiah's normally stern face as he thought of Havivah; in her short days she had sent so many accursed Hebrew dogs back to the pit where they belonged. Once she had conducted a ceremony that lasted all night, and during it she had sacrificed twenty false Hebrew prophets to Baal! So much for the pitiful Hebrew God. . . .

"Surely we shall overcome all," Abiah said to himself, "With Baal on our side, who can beat us?"

He drew himself up taller and unsheathed his sword from its scabbard. As he turned the weighted blade in his hand, Abiah admired the honed metal edge of the dark weapon. Soon this edge would taste the blood of the Hebrews.

Abiah's thoughts were interrupted by Haskel, his second-in-command.

"My lord," Haskel said quietly, giving a salute. "Ah, yes, Haskel," Abiah replied warmly, turning to face the younger man, "How fare the troops?"

"Well, my lord," Haskel stammered, shifting his weight from one foot to the other nervously, "they . . . are . . . well . . . good, that is, sir," he gave a nervous twitter of a laugh and a half-bow, "but the lady . . . Priestess Havivah . . . she is distressed. She–she would speak with you, my lord."

Abiah re-sheathed his blade, smiling in satisfaction as the heavy metal clanged home. "Bring her to me," he ordered, "But make sure no one slows his ship, even by a cubit per hour, or I shall treat him as a Hebrew!"

Haskel bowed fully this time. "I hear and obey, my lord," he mumbled, hurrying away to fetch Havivah.

The ascetic man watched Haskel walk away, his mind already in battle mode.

He gave a small, nearly inaudible sigh, and looked back out into the ocean. The deathly silent water looked as bleak as his mood was becoming. How long he stood there staring, Abiah did not know. But stare he did, with a tight frown on his face. The water was so black, so hopeless, and so impenetrable. For all he knew, they could be sailing over an unfathomed abyss now.

A shiver of fear shook his normally resolute being; this stretch of water struck terror in him—terror from his very soul, it seemed. He felt a tremble course through him as the water reflected in his eyes. Stilling his tremors, he remained lost in thought.

"It is well and good to fear," a mystical voice spoke up from behind Abiah, "There is much evil here."

Abiah turned to see Havivah, the Priestess of Baal. She pulled her silken scarf tighter around her shoulders and boldly walked up to Abiah's side. Her low-cut, scarlet gown did nothing to protect her from the cold air, and she shivered.

"Baal is not feared here, Abiah," she whispered, her gaze distant, "but I can feel *its* presence."

Mesmerized, Abiah stared at Havivah for a moment, completely lost under her spell. Her voice held an accent none of them had ever heard before, and she was exotically beautiful; most men, Abiah included, believed her to be some sort of goddess herself.

"What do you mean by 'it,' Lady Havivah?" Abiah asked slowly, his eyes never straying from her mysteriously calm face. He felt halfway in a dream as he drank in her beauty, but her next words shocked him fully awake in an instant.

"You do not know what you feel?" she laughed cynically, a half-smile gracing her face, "It is *Death*, mighty man. Death. . . . Can you fight with Death and win? No man has in over two thousand years of life!" Then she turned abruptly and glided away, the scent of her perfume lingering only moments after her departure.

And just like that, every bit of hope left Abiah's body. He doubled over as if in pain, clutching the rail so tightly he nearly crushed it. His breath came in heavy, short gasps as pervasive despair wound its way through his pores and into his very soul.

And then it came. A roar split the air, sounding like the very demons of hell were at his gate! A blast of fire welled up from the water, engulfing the ship in a matter of moments. Perhaps this *was* hell! All of the ships were incinerated in less than thirty seconds, leaving behind only a few scattered ashes and one partially charred, yet barely alive man.

As the survivor, more corpse than man, floated in the dark sea, he tried to draw his weapon. He would *not* go down without a fight! But it was useless. The dark shape moved quickly through the ruins, making quick work of the only survivor: Abiah. No, the mighty man could not fight Death and win.

XXXX

It scanned the depths with its yellow eye, so full of malice and hate that it could barely see.

'Yet again I prevailed. . . . Their Baal was powerless against Death,' it thought with pride; it would have even smiled, had it been able to do so.

'But I do wish people would not mention that . . . that . . . Hebrew God. . . .' It thought, shuddering for some reason unknown even to it.

Slowly Azrael sank back to the floor and fell asleep, confident in its victory and security.

X 300 B.C. X

"Kyros, please turn back," Dessa pleaded, grabbing her husband's arm, "This unnatural dark is a bad omen!"

"Nonsense, Dessa," Kyros snapped, pushing her away, "You worry too much." He shook his head, going back to his work on the mainsail.

"But Poseidon is angry!" Dessa whimpered, falling to her knees on the deck.

Kyros shook his head, muttering an oath under his breath. "Silly, superstitious female," he grumbled, shooting her a withering look, "you know I don't believe in such things. But if I *did*, what would be bad luck would be to let this head wind pass by. . . . *grunt*. . . . All right, let's sail. . . . Wait. Where did the wind go?"

He dropped the rope from his hands, letting it slide slowly to the ground like a limp snake. Their small caravel was now dead in the water, surrounded by the suffocating shadow.

"Noooo," Dessa wailed, beginning to cry as she rocked back and forth, "Zeus! Oh, Zeus! Save us! No, no. . . . Hades is coming!"

Kyros ignored his frantic wife and strode to the front of their tiny vessel. Lifting an oar, he tried in vain to paddle the boat.

"We're not going anywhere until a good, stiff breeze come up," he grumbled after a minute, "I should have built a smaller boat." (They were only poor peasants and could not afford slaves to row their boat; it required at least five people to propel it, though it was small.) "The planets had aligned," he muttered to himself, going back to the rigging and pulling a rope tighter, "I thought for sure a heavy breeze was to follow. . . ."

"Kyros," Dessa whispered gently, laying her slender hand on her husband's broad shoulder, "Please, let's turn back! Surely Zeus will hear our cries and send us a strong win-"

"Shah, woman," Kyros spat, backhanding her across the face, "speak not of the gods again in my presence!" He glared at her, then spun on his heel and stomped to the back of the boat, muttering angrily under his breath.

Dessa lifted a trembling hand to her swollen cheek, then fell to her knees, tear after tear rolling silently down her thin face. She let her head droop forward until it came to rest on the mast.

"He'll never turn back," she whispered, covering her face with her hands, "We're doomed!" Through teary eyes she watched, only slightly stunned, as something black and leathery inched over the side of the boat.

"Kyros," she began timidly, her voice strangled from crying. But she never got to finish her sentence.

Crack! The boat exploded, wood flying everywhere.

Dessa screamed as she flew through the air; she hit the water hard and her cries were instantly silenced by a slimy, thick, living rope.

It scanned the decimated wreck lazily as it choked Dessa's corpse, then plunged downward into the pit below, savoring the feel of bloody water trickling over its hide.

'I win yet again,' Azrael gloated, 'Their gods were weaklings too. Death still rules!' He gripped Dessa's body tighter and settled onto the jagged stone floor with a smirk.

X A.D. 0 X

The small fishing boat tossed wildly in the waves, nearly capsizing one moment and nearly sinking the next.

"We have to get out of this storm!" Simon yelled, grabbing onto the side of the boat, "Aim for that cave!" Thomas grabbed at the wildly flapping sail and struggled to hold it. "We probably won't make it," he muttered gloomily, but he pulled the ropes taut anyway.

Underneath the violent waves Azrael swam slowly, carefully eyeing the boat. 'I think a few more waves should do it,' it mused, sending a bolt of electricity through the water to create larger swells, 'Idiots! It is useless to resist. You will soon drown by my might!' It muttered some foul words under its breath, strengthening the squall.

By now the waves were breaking over the boat, and the men inside truly believed they were going to drown! Well, twelve of them did; the thirteenth lay in the back of the boat, sleeping peacefully.

"We're going down, Simon!" Andrew yelled to his brother, "I've never seen a storm this bad in all of my days as a fisherman!" Simon nodded ruefully, grabbing the side of the boat to steady himself.

The boat careened to one side as the creature forced more water to churn about the tiny craft with more evil words. In only a few minutes it planned to claim its next prize! But what it had not planned on was the thirteenth Man in the boat. . . .

XXXX

A huge wave rose over the boat; it broke fiercely, nearly swamping the craft. "Bail!" Andrew ordered, beginning to shovel water back out of the boat, "And somebody wake the Master up!" He continued to bail energetically, his muscles straining at every bucketful of water he tossed out of the craft.

Thomas dropped the bucket that he had been bailing with and staggered toward the stern of the boat, nearly falling over twice. Once as he hit the side, he thought he saw a large, black shadow underneath the vicious waves, but he did not stop to ponder about it. Finally he reached his destination—the rear of the boat—where Jesus was sleeping peacefully on a cushion.

"Teacher!" Thomas screamed to be heard over the howling wind and rain, "Don't you care that we're going to die?"

Jesus sat up, fully awake now, and merely looked at Thomas. Then He stood and addressed the storm.

XXXX

Azrael whipped the water around faster and faster, intensifying the storm to the fullest extent of its abilities. 'Any moment now, they will fall out!' it hissed in anticipation, pouring its pure fury into the waves and lightning.

The angry spells it spoke writhed upwards, building the storm until Azrael nearly lost control itself. But it managed to hang onto the reins as the storm built and built, fueled by its dark soul.

Every word it spat caused the clouds to slowly grow. They inched downward like fingers from the sky, stretching out, reaching to crush the ship between sky and beast. Now the boat was literally between the Devil and the deep blue sea.

The beast shot one tentacle up, ready to obliterate the men. It hissed a few words to stupefy them, rendering them dullards. Now, when they were absolutely helpless, it attacked!

But suddenly a Voice thundered out, "Silence! Be still!"

Instantly, white hot pain shot through Azrael. 'CURSE YOU!' it tried to scream, but Death was mute and powerless. It could not move forward or backward. Light was everywhere; holy, pure light from that *Man*!

The storm was finished, over, done. Azrael shrieked again and again with its silent voice, writhing in pain as it sank back down to the darkness below, leaving the men untouched and the ocean as smooth as glass.

In the presence of the Fisherman, Death found it had no power. How was this possible!?

X A.D. 1400 X

The canoe shot swiftly through the water, slicing it as cleanly as a knife. Six braves, faces as blank and hard as stone walls, paddled the canoe silently.

Chief Waban stood board straight in the front of the boat, his dark eyes absorbing his surroundings. The tall eagle feather in his headdress kept the braves silent; this man had faced many dangers to retrieve that feather and he was not to be questioned.

This mission could, in no way, shape, or form, be more dangerous than his journey for the feather, the Chief had told his men. For any of them to speak out now would be great dishonor; not one brave would risk it.

And so they paddled: silently; quickly; obediently. Waban's tall visage encouraged them as well. Not only was he very courageous, but he was also good medicine. Very close to the Great Spirit and brother nature, Waban led his men wisely. His men felt no fear or anxiety, for their chief said the spirits were pleased.

And so the canoe pressed onward toward its demise . . . or so Azrael planned.

XXXX

A shadow bled across the water beneath the canoe, barely visible in the inky blackness. Azrael stared upward from beneath the waves, waiting patiently.

Green-tinged light wafted outward from its large, spherical eye, making its fangs glow in the eerie aura. The light settled on the bottom of the wooden vessel, marking a single figure for the first hit.

A low growl emanated from its maw, but other than that it remained very quiet. The prey must not know they were being hunted.

XXXX

Chief Waban turned his head slightly and barked the command to stop. Instantly the canoe ground to a halt in the water. "I know not this water," Waban mused, gripping his bow tightly, "Be ready to fight, Warriors." Then he gave a short nod and once again the canoe rushed forward.

But before they could travel even a yard, a screech split the air, raising the hair on the back of Waban's neck.

The last brave in the canoe made a strange sound, then collapsed forward, headless. Blood spurted from his severed arteries, spattering the occupants of the canoe.

"Paddle!" the chief yelled, shoving the decapitated body out of the canoe.

Instantly another brave dropped, also headless. Blood was flowing wildly now, running in tiny rivers down the canoe's curved sides and pooling in the floor. The men began to panic as their feet were covered in an inch of blood; they rowed frantically, their strokes erratic and uncoordinated.

But it was no good: no man can outrun Death. A few minutes later, a blood-filled canoe floated on the icy waters, spinning slowly in the weak current. From the Abyss below, it watched in delight.

'Once again, all gods bow to me!' it thought in sheer glee, 'Death can conquer all!' It was getting cocky now, beginning to forget the humiliating Fisherman incident. Azrael slipped up to the canoe, tipped it back boldly, and drank the blood in one gulp.

X A.D. 1996 X

Alyssa giggled, teetering drunkenly. "Whoa, the ship's moving," she slurred, collapsing onto a deck chair with a stupid grin, "Sho, Mikey, whatcha' doin' tonight?"

"We–ell," Michael drawled, drawing the world out into two syllables, "It's like this, hon: first the bar's calling me, then the boys 'n' me are gonna play a little card game, and after that," he gave a shrug, "I guess we'll see, won't we? Maybe another round at the bar."

"Excuse me, Miss, Sir," a voice with a thick Scottish accent interrupted them, "but I'll have ta ask ye ta go below decks. We've spotted something fairly strange on our radars, and we're not quite sure what it is. It's movin' in at a fairly fast clip, so we're goin' ta try'n outrun it."

"Thanks, Captain O'Heen," Michael said, taking Alyssa by the shoulders, "We're so gone."

"Thank ye, laddie," the old captain sighed, his voice sounding tired. Somehow he sensed that this was far from over.

XXXX

"Sir, we're moving at thirty-four knots, and the object is overtaking us like–like we're standing still!" the first mate informed Captain O'Heen frantically, "What are your orders?"

"We've got ta hide," Captain O'Heen decided, running a hand through his graying hair, "Set course for that cave over there."

The huge cruise ship, the *Emerald Day*, swung slowly toward the cave and slipped in. Now all that they could do was to wait. Hours passed and nothing happened. Slowly the crew began to relax, feeling that their scare was over; the casinos reopened, and Michael and his buddies started a drinking game.

But Captain O'Heen was not fooled. "It's still there," he murmured to himself as he stared out into the sinfully black sky, "It knows where we are." He bowed his head in thought, but there was no solution. If the *Emerald Day* stayed put, they would become a sitting duck and eventually it would find them; if they ran, it would overtake and catch them.

"Ye cannot escape, laddie," the captain told himself sadly, "This'll be the end of ye, O'Heen. . . . But I'll not go down in here! Nay, Captain Brogan O'Heen will go down honorably."

The old man pulled his body up, then walked out onto the deck as one doomed. He took the helm again, called out an all-clear, and allowed the ship to sail on to its death.

Less than half an hour later, blood-curdling screams and cries decorated the air as the *Emerald Day* slowly sank into the water. Tentacles wrapped tightly around the ship, squeezing the very life from its engines.

The creature sent a pulse of energy through the ship, crossing the wires from the engine room. The *Emerald Day* lit up briefly with a hissing sound, and then burst into a raging inferno. The black waters lapped at the sides of the ship, but refused to quench the flames.

Finally the rooms all filled with the heavy water and the *Emerald Day* slipped below the water line and sank into the depths.

Azrael seemed to laugh, mocking the cruise ship's demise as the derelict settled into the graveyard below. 'I win again,' it thought, 'and no wonder. These people were their own gods. *Pathetic*!'

X A.D. 2020 X

"Move!" Falcon ordered, lifting his Barrett M98B sniper rifle to stare down the barrel. The recoil-operated .50 BMG gun was capable of killing quickly, something Falcon liked. He checked his rifle for readiness, and sat back into his seat.

The sub shot through the depths like a bullet, its floodlights barely piercing the extreme darkness. It was composed of a lightweight, extremely durable titanium alloy and was equipped with enough atomic weapons to nuke the whole world twice over.

Occupying the sub were one hundred men, each one a weapon in his mind-set and body. They had trained for years before even setting foot on this sub, and each one carried M16A4 guns . . . two of them per man.

They also had an array of knives, ranging from switchblades to KA-BARs. They could run on Epinephrine for days without rest; they fought wounded or half-dead as well as they did completely uninjured. They were called the Death Hawks.

Their motto? 'Do not mess with us, or we will mess you up.'

XXXX

"Target: Kraken. Objective: locate and destroy," Falcon growled, his coal-black eyes staring into the even-blacker waters.

He clenched his jaw, the scar down his left cheek whitening. His claw-like nails tapped on the table, nicking pieces out of the deep cherry wood. The scars left behind were his mark; even if he died today, all would know that Falcon had killed the Kraken. The door to his private chamber burst open, but Falcon continued his vigil, his fingers gouging deeper into the fine wood.

"Sir!" Maddox called, saluting sharply, "We found it!"

Falcon refused to even turn and face his subordinate. "Ready the nukes," he hissed, cocking his head like an eagle, his dark black locks of hair falling to one side, "Let's go kick som–"

Suddenly the sub began shaking violently, knocking Maddox and Falcon to the floor. Falcon, rifle still clutched tightly in his clawed hand, crashed into the edge of the desk, the wood now gouging him. "Fire!" he cursed, wiping a trickle of blood from the corner of his mouth, "Fire you idiots!"

Moments later they head a *whoosh* as twenty tons of nuclear weapons fired directly into the creature. A shockwave scuttled across the water until the still-silent darkness engulfed it. Lights flashed wildly as the bombs found their target.

Maddox flinched as the shockwave blasted into their sub, wondering for a moment how well-constructed their vehicle actually was. Finally everything went still, and a cheer rang out from the Death Hawks. They had won!

Falcon pushed himself off the floor, barely believing what had just happened. "We beat it," he murmured, holding onto the railing as if it were his life-line, "We . . . won." He ran a hand through his hair, feeling the pain in his mouth slowly begin to subside as victory numbed his whole body. The blood trickling down his face no longer stung.

"We won!" he roared, throwing up his fist in a victory salute. His excitement spread faster than anthrax throughout the mini-sub. The Death Hawks were too excited to notice danger now.

When the hatch began to slowly inch around with a metallic creak, it went unnoticed. The hatch paused momentarily as the creature feared discovery. Still the celebration rang out loudly, so it continued boldly opening the metal portal.

Suddenly the hatch flew open and water and tentacles surged into the machine. Falcon was the first to notice as a tentacle wrapped around his leg.

"Fire!" he screamed, ripping off the tip of the Kraken's arm with his bare hands. He raised his Barrett M98B and let loose with a volley of bullets, but the gun slipped from his blood-soaked hands.

Maddox leapt up and fired off several rounds into the beast, but the bullets passed through the animal as if it were liquid or . . . or a ghost.

Men threw down their guns and drew their knives, but they never got the opportunity to use the weapons. A wave of fire blasted through the sub, splitting it down the middle like a wet sheet of paper and incinerating the metal walls.

Not one Death Hawk had a chance.

XXXX

It settled on the bottom, quite content.

'Their weapon gods were futile,' Azrael reveled, 'I am everything! You cannot outrun Death . . . you cannot hide from Death . . . you cannot fight Death and win forever. . . . Sooner or later, every mortal will face Death, and Death will win. The only ones that got away were the friends of that lowly Fisherman. None of the others were ready to meet Death.'

XXXX

Are *you* ready?

James 4:14 – 'How do you know what your life will be like tomorrow? Your life is like the morning fog—it's here a little while, and then it's gone.' NLT

Luke 12:20 – 'But God said to him, "You fool! This very night your soul is required of you; and now who will own what you have prepared?"' NAS

John 3:16 – 'For God loved the world so much that He gave His one and only Son, so that everyone who believes in Him will not perish but have eternal life.' NLT

Confident Christianity is proud to present the 2009

Dorothy Sayer's Award

to

Kimberly Hanson

Waikoloa, HI

Second Place

(category: High School)

Bio: The first time I was inspired to seriously write a story was in the 6th grade when I found out my younger brother was going to be writing a novel for school. Little did I know that upon starting to write that story, I had embarked on a journey that would open a new world to me as I slowly realized that I loved the art of writing.

Each time I created a new twist in a story I had a thrill, and soon all I wanted to do was write stories with captivating plots while incorporating morals throughout the excitement. As I continued to write, I found that through writing I could glorify God and therefore unite two of my passions together into one ultimate blaze of fulfillment.

I hope to write worthwhile stories for the rest of my life, but I give God the glory for any fiber of talent in my being, knowing that it was all woven together by Him. Thank you, Jesus.

Way Out West

by Kimberly Hanson

Copyright 2009, All Rights Reserved

A burly, coarse looking man sat at his large wooden table eagerly reading through a thick letter. His interest increased as he flipped through the pages with a flicker in his dark eye; his wife, who stood in the background, seemed apparently curious as well, her glance often falling upon him. She busied herself with dishes as her husband came to the closing of the last filled sheet.

Slapping down the paper with a satisfied air, Rodger Hemmingway grinned to his wife.

"Now are you gonna tell me what Anne said or just look at me so?" Betsey asked, turning to him with a provoked countenance.

"Ah, yes, dear, I'll tell ya; don't ya be angry at me now. Anne and Sam are makin' the journey from the east. They expect to be here round a few weeks." Rodger smiled.

"They're coming to Bern Town?" Betsey cried, dropping a dish in her astonishment.

"Ay, Bern Town fo' sure. Anne says they can't help wantin to settle here after what we've told her bout it. And she says she's hopin to live near some family, and as we's the closest family they have in these parts, they're comin here—out to Bern Town."

"I say, won't that be grand!"

Rodger only nodded in agreement as he gathered up the sheets of the letter. Carefully folding them up, he placed them in a small drawer in the only desk they had in their house.

After having moved out west five years ago, Rodger and his wife had experienced severely hard times. They had made their livelihood off of growing corn and wheat, which had only brought in enough money to survive for his family of four. His two daughters Elizabeth and Patricia had known hard work and suffering despite their young age, for their father needed them to work, and work they did. Both parent's hearts were sore with the suffering they could have endured very well on their own, but having to see their own children have to bear with poverty was the ultimate punishment.

"But, Rodger, when whas that letter written?" Betsey asked suddenly.

"D'say bout three weeks ago."

"Three weeks? And they've been travelin for a few already, I s'pose?"

"Ay, dear,"

"Then they should be here sooner then they say—been travelin for many, many weeks probably! We'll have them at our doorstep in less then a fortnight if I donno any better." She said, smiling to her husband as wrinkles formed around her mouth and eyes. Her careworn face and sunburned skin evidence of all of the long hours of toil and labor she had spent outdoors.

"You're almost always right, dear, and I don't doubt yor word."

Rodger waited eagerly for his sister Anne's arrival along with her husband and three children, Anne having been his greatest companion through his hard youth. His life as a child had been as hard as his life in the west, if not harder, for they had been a poor, large family who had had to resort to crime for most of their food. Rodger was not proud of his past, however, and had come to know the Good Lord when he grew older, which had resorted in his decision to move out west with his new family. Unsure of his dear sister's future, Rodger had left only to hear the news that she was married to an honest man and was out of danger from dying of the grueling life she had once known.

Anne's husband Sam was not a rich man, though, and was apt to wish to explore the west and all of its mysteries. Anne could have not objection and they had started off in a state of indefiniteness.

Through all of this, Rodger had been more delighted then he dared show, and kept his secret-joy to himself for his own pleasure and excitement.

Nevertheless, a month passed with no sign of Anne, though a large bundle had arrived in their place.

It was a heavy wooden box, sealed tightly as if to ensure that nobody, including himself, could get at it. The only way Rodger was able to open it was with a sledge hammer. He shattered the wood into splinters and after removing a few bundles of blankets beheld seven golden nuggets, each heavy and brilliant.

"Betsy! Betsy! Darlin! Come here!" Rodger hollered from outside.

His wife came running out of the small house, breathless; her face flushed and fearful.

"Oh! What's 'appened? Are ye hurt?" She cried uneasily as she ran down the steps and rushed to his side.

"No, but look ye here! Look at what Anne's sent us!" He cried, holding up a few of the nuggets in amazement.

"Is it what I see? No! Yes? Oh! Can it be true?" She exclaimed in disbelief.

"If you see th' same thin I do, it must be—!"

"Gold!" Betsey whispered, apprehensive that anyone else might hear.

"Gold, indeed, my dear. I wouldn't a believed it unless I'd see'd it and here she is!"

"But, now, what's Anne a'thinkin sendin' us such thins? Where on earth did they find it?" Betsey asked, digging through the wood impatiently and flinging blankets into the air, hoping to find some sort of explanation.

"We ha' better bring this all inside before someone sees us. If anyone finds out bout this problems could come up." Rodger said, gathering the blankets his wife had strewn about, wrapping the gold nuggets in them and staring suspiciously about the expanse of land.

"Yor right, dear," Betsey gasped, trying to cover up their tracks by kicking the bit of wood that remained from the box into a corner and running around like a wild woman, as if she had lost her sanity.

"Betsy, go into th' house 'fore you start goin out o' yor wits an' take the blankets with ya." Rodger ordered, a bit worried for her.

She obeyed quickly and ran into the house only to be accosted by her two daughters who were excited to find out what Aunt Anne had sent. Betsey was so mortified by them in her agitation that she ordered them to go to their rooms and stay in there! Elizabeth and Patricia, so unused to their mother being taken into fits, obeyed her anxiously.

"What's goin on in here that yor yellin at the girls so? I could right hear ya from outside." Rodger exclaimed, entering the house.

"But we can't let 'em see what we've got! They'll go tellin' it to everyone in town!" Betsey defended, still crazed by shock.

"Sit ye down and don't glance at the gold if it's gonna make you so." Rodger chided, as if his wife were a child "Now, I've found a letter 'mong the trash—"

"A letter!"

"A letter and I'll read it to ya ta calm ye for you seem right mad! Listen.

My Dear Rodger and Betsey,

Providence has sent Sam and me a fortune. While passin' through Missouri we came upon an old man and his wife who were also traveling to the west. While we traveled with em they became ill with the fever and begged us to help them on their way back to the Carolina's. Sam didn't want to, for it would delay us more then we liked, but they offered to pay us such a deal o' money that we coudn't deny em. After aidin' em home, we couldn't believe all of the thins they gave us, including the nuggets we've sent you. Sam said it would be wiser to send you some o' it 'cause if people found out that we had such a fortune they'd surely be after us and our family. We have enclosed seven golden nuggets and hope you will keep them safe. Don't you nor Betsey tell anyone that you 'ave them, for it could mean a deal o' trouble for all o' us, but Sam has devised a plan so wait till we arrive. Until then.

Yours truly, Anne'

There now, Betsey, that's the plan."

"It sounds sensible." She answered softly, having gained back all of her senses and comprehending the whole of the letter.

They both agreed to hide the gold in a deep hole in the middle of their barn where they hoped nobody would find it.

After a few more weeks another letter arrived from Anne who said they were near Bern Town and expected to arrive soon. Rodger was elated and decided to take a day to go into town and gather some things.

"Good mornin', Sheriff," Rodger bowed as he rode along in his small buggy.

"An' ta ya, Mr. Hemmin'way," The Sheriff nodded.

Rodger stopped his horse and tied him up as he leapt out of his buggy.

"He's been moppin' 'bout town nearin' a week I'd sa'" Mr. Walker observed, nodding towards a small shed where a dirty young man sat.

"Who's the boy?" Rodger asked, joining the conversation.

"Nobody knaws. He just wandered inta town—never talks to nobody." Mr. Walker replied.

"You keepin' an eye on him, Sheriff?" Mr. Davis asked darkly.

"Ay, Mr. Davis, there ain't notin' to worry 'bout. He don't want na harm." Sheriff said.

"How d' ye knaw? Them tramps is always causin' trouble round these parts." Mr. Davis frowned.

"Well, I'll keep a' eye on him; donna ya worry." Sheriff smiled, amused.

Rodger bought all of his items, and after glancing at the men, he walked over to the tramp that seemed dozing off with his hat over his eyes.

"Son," Rodger said, stepping towards him.

The boy made no response.

"Eh, son, ya awake?"

"Huh?" The boy jerked, pulling his hat from his dusty face and starting up in fright.

"No need ta be afraid. I just wanna speak ta ya." Rodger said.

"What's it?" The boy asked, standing up and dusting himself off.

"Ya 'ave a place to stay?"

"Reckon not,"

"When's the last time ya had a good meal?"

"Can't say I've ever had one, dependin' on what ya calls a good meal." He said, looking at him incredulously.

"Then ye'll have no objection to havin' one? You look right starved and my wife'll be happy to cook up a hardy meal for ya."

"Uh…"

"My buggy's right there and my home not far. Come along." Rodger said, plodding over to his buggy while smirking at his stunned comrades. The utter thought that he should invite such a dangerous guest to his house was insane.

While this went on the boy had no option but to snatch up his sack and follow.

As Rodger walked past, Mr. Davis gripped his arm and whispered menacingly, "Ya donno what yor doin invitin' a tramp ta yor house."

Rodger only nodded to them and started off with boy by his side. When they arrived home both Elizabeth and Patricia eyed the young man curiously. It was the first time their father had ever brought home a stranger.

The boy hopped out of the carriage and took out his sack, glancing around.

"What's yor name, son?" Rodger asked as he put the buggy away.

"Jimmy," He answered, aiding Rodger.

"What ar' ya doin' wanderin' around a small town like this for?" Rodger asked bluntly.

"Just passin' thro'. I'll be leavin' soon."

"Where ta?"

"Donno, but I'll be leavin'"

"That's rather unusual for a boy o' yor age, travelin' round so. What's yer age?"

"I'd say round sixteen—I think."

"How'd ya get to not knowin' yor own age?"

"Never kep' track, that's all." Jimmy said defensively.

Rodger only nodded and walked out of the barn and towards the house.

Betsey had seen the unusual visitor from the window and eyed Rodger inquisitively. He only answered with a smile as he brought the guest in.

"This here's Jimmy, dear. I've invited him for dinner." Rodger said.

Betsey acknowledged Jimmy and then turned towards Rodger, expecting more.

"Where're ya from, Jimmy?" Betsey asked after a long pause.

"No where parti'larly. I travel 'round."

"Well, yor welcome to have supper with us. I'm preparin' it now." Betsey said, turning back to the kitchen.

"Thank ye, mum," Jimmy said, also turning around and going towards the door. Rodger followed him, and soon found himself in the barn as he watched Jimmy settle down on the haystack and begin getting back into the same posture he had found him—the first preparation being to put his hat over his face.

Rodger made no comment and went back to the house slowly.

"What ar' ya doin, Rodger, invitin' a boy here fo' supper when ya know we're expectin' Anne here any day now." Betsey scolded once he was back.

"Well, now, I noticed he was on th' street and so forlorn lookin'—I couldn't just leave 'im there wi' all the town being suspicious of him."

"Yes ya could've."

"There now, he'll only be here fo' supper and perhaps spend a night in th' barn. Besides, dear, he said he was passin' through."

"Have yor way of it, Rodger, but I am awful uneasy 'bout it. Perhaps people've a reason for being suspicious o' him? And ya know wat we keep in th' barn and wat if he were ta find it? Keep a sharp eye on him, and pray he don't find that treasure." Betsey said, her eyes beginning to flash and her hands to work faster.

"Perhaps I'd better tell 'im not to stay." Rodger suggested.

"No, that would not be good—invitin' him one moment and gettin' rid o' him th' other—no, it wouldn't be proper. One night in the barn and then he must go."

They had a silent dinner that night, all watching in amazement as Jimmy ate his meal. He swallowed up everything with startling speed and with no impediments such as manners to block his way. The food was neither elegant nor plentiful, but potatoes and a few vegetables was enough to gratify they tramp, and he thanked them in a profusion of words before going back to the barn for the night.

The next morning Jimmy was up early, his hair filled with twigs and a piece of straw balancing in his mouth as he slowly chewed at it. Spotting Rodger on the veranda, he treaded over to him.

"Yor up mighty early. It's not a quarter past four." The stout farmer said, staring at the tramp with his steady black eyes.

"Yes, weel, my afternoon naps help me ta wake up early." Jimmy said, kicking at the ground aimlessly. Lifting his downcast face Jimmy stuffed his hands in his pockets and straightened his back. "I'll be leavin' today right afta breakfast."

"I see. If ye don't mind me askin' where are ye goin'?" Rodger asked.

"I wanna make my way back east. Can't stand the west no longer."

"That's a long journey." Rodger said, surprised at the young boy's ridiculous answer. He didn't look like he could possibly pay his way there, and Rodger, tightening up his fists and clenching his jaw in fear, hoped he hadn't discovered the gold, which would surely cover all expenses and still leave him a fortune afterwards.

"I want ta make me way back ta th' cities an' work in an office or somethin'." Jimmy said, a bit embarrassed at his answer, for why would a tramp like him want to work in an office—it didn't seem to suit at all.

Rodger made no answer but only stood there for a while, his mind racing as he thought of a way to find out whether Jimmy had found the gold or whether what he was saying was simply a fancy or, possibly, a lie. Turning to go into the house, Rodger made an unintelligible comment about Betsey cooking and ran into his room, almost knocking the hinges off the door, he was so clumsy and overcome.

He ran into Betsey, who was making the bed, and exclaimed, "Betsey, oh, dear, ya was right! He's done and found the gold an' wat am I to do?!" He cried, pulling at his hair in agony.

"Found it? Oh, but how do ya knaw? Is he gawn? Has he taken and run?!" Betsey sobbed, tears already filling her eyes.

"Hush, dear, no, he's not gawn—he's in the house! Talk softly.

But, now, ye must get 'im away so that I can search for ware he's hid it—per'aps he's hid it in that sack he's been carrin' round. Come now, let's make a plan." Rodger said, eagerly sitting down in a large rocking chair and beginning to sway fiercely.

After viciously rocking for a few minutes he and Betsey decided that she would make breakfast and while they ate she would beg Jimmy to come with her and the girls to the fields where they expected to find wild strawberries, saying that they needed help getting across the river. It was the best plan they could devise in the short time they had, and, after composing themselves, both came out of their room.

Jimmy was instantly ready for breakfast and ate it with as much ferocity as he had eaten his dinner the previous night.

After speaking to each other with their eyes Betsey finally stuttered out her question.

"Pick strawberries?" Jimmy asked, his face revealing his amazement at such an incredible question.

"Yes; I know it's rather a queer question, but we'd need yor help crossin' th' river an' then getttin' back home." Betsey said, attempting with all her strength to not seem desperate.

"An' I could save a days work 'cause usually I go out wi' 'em. A day's work is worth a lot fo' us farmers, and I'd be mighty grateful to ya." Rodger said.

Jimmy looked at his empty plate and then at Betsey and Rodger. "I s'ppose it's th' least I culd do for ye for th' meals ye've given me." He said, standing up.

"Thank ye," Betsey said, trying to suppress her joy.

The girls soon awoke afterwards and after eating, the four of them went off to the fields, each carrying a basket on one arm with Jimmy trailing behind them awkwardly.

It took every bit of self control for Rodger to not run into the barn once they were a few yards away, but, making sure they were only specks in the distance before he attempted it, Rodger slowly made his way into the barn. After searching around the haystack he found Jimmy's brown sack.

Grabbing it eagerly, he almost ripped it open, flinging the contents all around him. The first thing that he saw was a Bible, which he stared at in wonder, but tossing it aside, he snatched up a few pieces of jewelry. They looked valuable. One was a gold chain with diamonds, another was a golden locket, not as valuable looking, and the third was a golden ring with a large blue gem. After gathering these in a small pile his eyes caught sight of a golden nugget which had been flung to his side. He seized it and recognized that it was identical in size to his own; his heart sank, and he now knew his suspicions that Jimmy had found the gold were correct.

Sighing and dropping the gold, Rodger realized that he would have to inform the Sheriff about the gold he had. And once the Sheriff found out about gold, there was no way of preventing the rest of the town from hearing about it, which would mean possible danger for his family seeing that many of the farmers around him were going though as many hardships as he was, and some would likely resort to stealing and possibly worse crimes to get out of poverty.

Feeling the full misfortune of this, Rodger gathered up all of the articles from Jimmy's sack and mused over them, picking up each item and examining it scrupulously. He flipped through the pages of the Bible and interestingly found them well worn and crumpled from constant use. Surprised at this, he opened it up to the front, hoping to find some sort of name. But the name he found was not the one he had expected.

Reeling back in horror, Rodger dropped the Bible, petrified and shaken. "How? Oh, how is it possible?" he cried, instantly picking the Bible back up and running through the pages. He soon recognized a neat, familiar handwriting trickled throughout the leaves. Returning to the front page, he re-read the same name over and over again, wondering how it was possible. "Anne Walters" was written in a careful hand in dark, definite ink, and no matter how he rubbed his eyes and no matter how many times he chafed at the letters of her name, wondering if they would disappear, the words never vanished and his eyes never failed him.

Becoming aware of something, Rodger began examining each article of jewelry again. The ring was not familiar to him, nor the diamond necklace, but, opening the golden locket he found a picture of a man with dark hair and a comical smile: it must be Sam. Rodger had received a picture of Anne and Sam taken on their wedding day, and the face of the young man in that picture had a striking resemblance to the more aged features of this older, more matured Sam. Putting the locket in his pocket and keeping the Bible tight in his hand, Rodger walked to the center of the barn and began digging in the area where he had hid the gold.

If one gold nugget was missing he would know that Jimmy had taken it—but if they all still remained in the safe confinement of the ground it meant that Jimmy had attained it from another source—from his sister Anne. But, why would he also have her Bible and locket? Rodger was left in bewilderment as he dug away the earth and reached the box filled with nuggets.

Opening it, he found all seven nuggets securely hidden in the box.

Attempting to collect his thoughts, Roger promptly re-buried the treasure, relieved that Jimmy had not found them, but still in a state of perplexity, for how could Jimmy have stolen the golden nugget from Anne?

After sufficiently covering his own treasure Rodger put Jimmy's things back in the sack, but he kept the Bible and locket. Just as Rodger had done this a hurrying of hoofs was heard approaching and Rodger, panicking, threw down the sack and hid the items under the hay. After considering for a moment, he dove into the hay, the agitation of the moment overtaking him.

"Rodger!" A loud, breathless man called from outside. Banging was heard, as the person rapped loudly on the front door. "Rodger? Betsey? Anyone home?"

After a few more yells Rodger was able to sufficiently recognize the voice of the Sheriff. Slowly crawling out of the hay he peeked through a knot hole and saw that it *was* the Sheriff. Considering it safe, Rodger answered.

"Yes, John, I can hear ya. Wat's taken ye over so?" Rodger asked, stalking out of the barn without realizing that he still had hay poking out from his hair and clothes.

However, the Sheriff seemed not to notice it either; he ran up to Rodger wildly, his face contorted in pain and pity.

"I's gotten a letter fro' the Sheriff o' Orville. It's told me dat—weel, ye read it yorself—" He said, handing him an envelope.

Rodger received in uncertainly and tentatively opened the already-broken seal. The contents read:

To the Sheriff John Martin of Bern Town:

I have recently been informed that a Mr. Sam and Anne Walters along with their three children have been robbed and murdered by a group of bandits on their way to Bern Town. A common group of bandits have been roaming around this area, pillaging a few farmers and many travelers of all they have. In some cases the victims survive. I'm sorry to say that in this case the victims were not as fortunate. I have heard that the Walter's had relatives in Bern Town and therefore am dispatching a letter to you directly.

From, Sheriff Tom of Orville

After running through the contents a few times Rodger folded up the letter, his features twitching uncontrollably. Holding the letter in his trembling hands Rodger stammered if he might keep it, which the Sheriff abruptly said yes to. Rodger put the letter in his pocket as his cheeks turned an ashy gray and his eyes filled overflowing with tears.

"I'm so sorry, Rodger, for yor sister and innocent family. My apologies to you an' yor wife, who I'm sure will grieve. I will leave ya to tell 'em." The Sheriff said, going back to his horse and slowly saddling the sturdy animal.

"John, wait!" Rodger said suddenly, running up to him and grabbing him by the arm. "What if I told ya I knaw one of th' bandits who did this to my sister and her family?" He cried, attempting to hold back his tears and steady his quivering chin.

"How can ye knaw one? What do ya mean, Rodger?" Sheriff cried, jumping off his horse.

"It's that boy I brought fro' th' town—Jimmy's his name and I found in his sack a few thins which I'm sure belong to my sister. Her Bible and her locket. I tell ye, he's one o' them murderers!" Rodger cried fiercely, curbing his language from what he wished to call Jimmy.

After showing the Sheriff all of his evidence the Sheriff had no other option but to believe Rodger and all that he said. They decided to wait until his wife and daughters came home with Jimmy and then unexpectedly turn on him and tie him up to bring to the jail until he had a trial.

After waiting most of the morning and afternoon in suspense, the forms of his wife and children were seen in the distance. Rodger warned the Sheriff and they both got ready for their covert attack. They both waited in the house, the Sheriff behind the door with rope ready to tie Jimmy up when he entered while Rodger secured a gun in case of emergency.

Steps were heard coming towards the house and soon the door was thrown open and Betsey entered with her two daughters trailing close behind her. Rodger and the Sheriff waited for Jimmy expectedly, but after a few moments his form was still not seen enter.

"Where's Jimmy?" Rodger whispered to his wife.

"Jimmy—he left us." Betsey faltered, putting down a nice basketful of strawberries on the table with a shaky hand.

"Left you?!" Rodger yelled wildly, grabbing Betsey by the arms and shaking her.

"Oh, dear! I'm so sorry, but I couldn't make 'im stay 'cause he said he was needin' to go an' wouldn't be persuaded! I really did try, dear, I did!" Betsey sobbed, turning her head away.

"Why'd he leave ya? Tell me, where'd he go?" Rodger cried, still having an iron grip on her arms and he was about to violently shake her again when the Sheriff came from behind the door and demanded that Rodger loosen his grip.

Rodger pushed her away and slammed his arm on the countertop, his face red as the devil. His daughters both stood in fright, for they had never seen their father in such a passion. When the Sheriff was about to hint for the girls to leave he found that both of them had already retreated into the depths of their room, crying in distress.

"Now, Rodger, gain a'hold o' yorself an' don't be hurtin' no one. We'll find that boy an' ya can count on it." The Sheriff said, throwing down the rope in defeat and thumping into a chair next to Betsey, who was still sobbing in grief.

"Now, Betsey, ya need to tell us whare dat boy went. Did he tell ye?" The Sheriff asked, trying to sound soothing, but his loud voice and usually rough mien didn't permit him to sound conciliatory.

"I don't knaw—all he said whas he needed t' go." Betsey wept.

"Compose yorself and we'll talk more—but not till ye stop yor cryin'."

After a few moments the Sheriff went on. "What were ya'll talkin' about 'fore he left?"

"He—" Betsey stopped for a moment and thought. "Well, he asked me wat my name was."

"Yor name?"

"Yes, and I said it was Mrs. Betsey Hemmin'way."

"An' what did he say after dat?"

"Nothing—he sorta store at me an' then said he needed to leave— I didn't knaw why. I had na idea why he'd take off so for na reason— but he wouldn't be persuaded an' I couldn't do nothin'" Betsey cried, her eyes filling again when she gave a glance at Rodger who was still fuming.

"What's that sound?" Rodger said, starting.

"A horse!" Betsey said, springing out of her chair and bounding to the door.

"No! It might be Jimmy an' we don't want ya ta get hurt!" The Sheriff said, stopping Betsey.

Rodger quickly put the gun he had under his shirt and the Sheriff made sure he had his own gun in his holster.

"Go into yor bedroom, Betsey, and don't ye come out unless yor called by me or Rodger. Ya hear?" The Sheriff asked, staring Betsey squarely in the eyes.

"Yes—but, oh, don't get hurt, dear, oh, dear, don't get hurt!" She cried, clinging to Rodger.

"Get ye in th' room 'fore he comes." Rodger said, giving Betsey a push and also thrusting a letter into her hand which he said to read.

Betsey didn't need to be told thrice; she obeyed and went into her room hastily.

They both waited anxiously from indoors, each peering out the window, only the tops of their heads observable from outside.

"He don't look so good." Rodger said, seeing that the man approaching was riding his horse unstably.

"Weel, it's fo' sure dat darn tramp. Murderer! We'll get 'im." The Sheriff said, gripping his gun and preparing for a fight.

"I don't think we'll need them guns; he looks ill. He's bloody! Look, there's a wound on his side and he's pale as death. Per'aps it's a trick—don't move an' we'll soon find out." Rodger advised.

They both examined Jimmy, who had reached the house; his head was buried in the animal's mane, his whole form looking limp, while his chest heaved with exhaustion. After staying in that posture for a few minutes, he unexpectedly slid off the horse and hit the ground in a lifeless heap, not appearing to breathe or move.

"He's dead." Rodger whispered, his breath leaving him.

"Naw, I still think he's pullin' a trick. Wait a bit longer." The Sheriff said, extremely apprehensive.

"I think he's dead, John. Look, he hadn't moved fo' the past five minutes." Rodger said, standing up and moving towards the door.

The Sheriff followed, his hand clutching his gun. They both walked slowly towards Jimmy, their guns now drawn and pointed. Being closer to him, they observed that he was breathing, though almost imperceptibly. They saw that a gun was fastened around Jimmy's waist in a holster, causing them to grip their own guns tighter and walk more gingerly. Once they were close enough, Rodger abruptly snatched the gun out of Jimmy's holster and threw it to the side, out of everyone's reach.

"Mr. Hemmi'nway," Jimmy wheezed, turning his head to face him; his eyes were dull and his face pallid as he suffered for breath.

"Jimmy, we've found ya out. We knaw what ya did." Rodger said, putting his gun away and kneeling down beside him.

"How?" Jimmy said, so weak that he couldn't show any emotion but pain.

"The items in yor sack told all. Now tell me wat 'appened to ya. How'd ya get shot?" Rodger asked, gazing at a large blood-soaked spot on his shirt. His clothes were ripped and soiled with dirt while blood was leaking from his lip and a black eye was setting in.

"I—" Jimmy attempted to speak but his strength gave way and his head sunk down limply. His chest still moved slowly, revealing that he had not yet left this world.

"Get 'im in th' house and we'll see wat we can do for 'im." The Sheriff said.

Rodger picked up the young boy's lifeless form and carried him into the house. Although he pitied him, a hard hatred was still in Rodger's heart through the knowledge that Jimmy had aided in the murder of his dear sister and her family.

Setting him on the table, Rodger called Betsey out of her room. When she came out her face seemed filled with a new heartache while her features showed pity. With a shriek, Betsey came to Jimmy's side and examined his wound and face grievously. Sorrowfully, she said he would probably not live because the wound was so severe and he had lost so much blood that it was a hopeless case.

"Take 'im inta our room and I'll try my best to nurse 'im, but I see no hope." Betsey said, and as Rodger began to lift Jimmy up again Betsey laid her hand on Rodger's arm and said softly, "I read the letter—"

But although Betsey had heard of Anne, she had never met her, and her grief could not be half the weight that Rodger held in his heart. Without responding to her words, Rodger took Jimmy into their room and when he came out he told Betsey at once to sit down and briefly revealed to her that Jimmy had been one of the bandits that had killed Anne.

Of course, Betsey could only be in disbelief and horror until the evidence was shown, the Bible and locket being undoubtedly strong evidence.

After this news Betsey sat in dismay for a few moments until she said, "I shall still nurse the guilty man, for Providence would not 'ave me be cruel and leave 'im in so much pain."

"'Course ya should nurse 'im, but, as ye said, he won't live a day." The Sheriff sneered.

"Only God knows that, Sheriff," Betsey said, getting some supplies ready for her work.

After a long night of nursing the invalid and trying to keep him from slipping into an everlasting sleep, Betsey awoke the next morning weak and tired from her constant post. Rodger camped in the living room, away from Jimmy. His anger against the young murderer was only intensified by the sleepless night, and although Rodger had not aided in nursing Jimmy, his strife against the boy had caused his head to ache through the night, not allowing his eyes to be closed in restful sleep for a moment.

"How is he?" Rodger asked the next morning when Betsey came out, looking tired and pale.

"Bad, but he's talkin' quite a bit. Askin' for water once in a while." She said, filling up a pitcher and going back into the bedroom.

Soon Elizabeth and Patricia awoke, both hungry and scared from the commotion of yesterday. Rodger told them they must stay outside that day and away from the house, making sure they didn't disturb Jimmy. Too scared to be disobedient, after breakfast the girls obeyed their father and went far into the fields.

"I wish to talk to 'im." Rodger said, coming into the room where Jimmy and his wife were.

"He can't talk much, dear, an' any type o' talkin' makes 'im weaker." Betsey said, alarmed at her husband's scowling face.

"He'll talk," Rodger said, grabbing a chair and seating himself next to Jimmy stoutly.

"I'll try," Jimmy said faintly, turning his colorless face towards Rodger. "I owe ye an explanation. I knaw my life is at it's end so I'll give ye my story, in th' last few words I'll ever speak."

Rodger seemed to bristle at the thought of Jimmy speaking of Anne, but, composing himself, he waited for the youth to catch his breath.

"I was one o' da bandits that pillaged yor sister. I was new in th' gang and wasn't prepared to kill no one—I only wanted some money to survive." He continued after a few minutes. "We found out dat yor sister's family had a lot o' money. We attacked 'em on their ways to Orville and I was th' one who made shore yor sister and chil'ren were held captive while they stole their goods." Jimmy caught his breath and with effort carried on. "Yor sister whas kind, and only begged dat we didn't hurt the chil'ren. They'd already killed her husband once we approached, 'cause he was shotin' at us. They got all o' th' money an' gold, but all th' while yor sister was speakin' to me o' God an' begging us ta be merc'ful. I decided as I watched 'er beggin' and cryin', dat I wouldn't never do it again." Wheezing desperately, Jimmy moaned from pain but perused his goal. "I never wanted ta hurt yor sister, but she grabbed my gun an' began firin' at us wen they said they was gonna kill th' chil'ren. After dat, they fired at her and then, th' poor kids, they killed 'em fo' no reason." Jimmy said, turning his face away in anguish.

Rodger blew into a passion, leaping upon Jimmy and grabbing is collar ferociously, mercilessly shaking him. "How could ya!" He cried lividly.

"Oh, Rodger, stop! Stop! He's gonna die soon and it's no use. Don't kill 'im, for then you'll be no better than he is right now. God forgive 'im!" Betsey said, upturning her face and weeping in silent prayer.

After Jimmy was released he took ten minutes to regain his bearings and breathe stably again. Finally, he continued, making no comment about Rodger's treatment, "I left th' bandits th' next day, escapin' wi' a gold nugget. I also took yor sister's Bible, fo' she had talked ta me a good deal while I sat wi' her and made me curious fo' it." Breathing deeply he carried on, "I haven't told ye yet how I got shot. When we was robbin' yor sister, we found out dat she'd given a good deal o' gold ta her relative's in Bern Town. We was gonna come here ta rob ya. I never thought o' tryin' ta save ya, but when I found out dat yor name was Hemmin'way and knew wat good folks ya was, I decided ta do somethin'. I went back ta Bern Town and wen I went there they was already here. I tried to convince 'em ta leave ya folks alone." After this lengthy speech it took Jimmy nearly double the time to regain strength, leaving both Betsey and Rodger in suspense. "But they wouldn't heed a word I spake, and soon got angry at me an' turned on me, but I managed ta get a gun an' shot back. We had a battle of it, but I won, fo' I'm a good shot." Jimmy attempted to smile, but was too weak. "I did it for yor family, sir, fo' yor own chil'ren, mum, dat they might not 'ave da same fate as those other poor innocents. I wish I never did it, and I wanted to return to the east where I might start over—but now I'm to die, but I die a Christian, for the Good Book which was yor sisters." Jimmy said, his voice leaving him. His death was not imminent. Jimmy was able to look into Betsey's eyes and thank her without words for her tedious care. Looking up at the ceiling, he wheezed out a few painful breaths, his face a grimace of agony. He moaned in anguish, until, suddenly, he stopped and, his features relaxing, his spirit was caught up into the air and he glided off to eternal happiness.

"Lord, is wat he has spoken true?" Betsey cried, her face streaming with tears as she fell on her knees in fervent prayer.

"Awful murderer! The worst o' sinners and the most wicked o' people, yor goin' to another place—not to peace." Rodger said ruthlessly, noticing that Jimmy had died.

"Rodger, no, no don't ye speak so. God only knaws such thins. Oh, how can ya say such thins, dear? Forgive—I thought ya had already forgiven 'im?" Betsey said, still crying.

"Forgive? What right has he ta be forgiven? He murdered Anne and th' rest o' em."

"He saved our family family from death and all ya show is bitterness."

"Killin' someone and then savin' us don't make him no better. He's a murderer and there ain't no other word I'll call him."

"If wat he said whas true he is a Christian."

"Stop justfyin' 'im, Betsey, or I'll start wonderin' wat's gotten into yor soft head!" Rodger yelled, infuriated.

"If ya don't forgive him wat can I think o' ya? Yor a strong Christian man, Rodger, and should forgive—you ain't no better then that murderer if ya don't forgive 'im. God wouldn't 'ave ya bein' bitter."

"How do ye expect me to forgive that boy after wat he did?"

"The same way Jesus forgave ya for all th' wrong thins we've all done."

Rodger stomped out of the room, not able to bear the sight of Jimmy's lifeless, upturned face. Betsey followed him out, and as they both paced around the room their eyes fell simultaneously on a piece of evidence lying in front of them—Anne's Bible.

The Sheriff soon came to the house and told them that a group of bandits had been found—all of them were dead, however a great deal of gold was found among their belongings, all of which would be forfeited to Rodger and Betsey once it was proven that it had been stolen from his murdered sister and family, for it was the same group of bandits Jimmy had killed and whom had robbed Anne.

In shock at the genuine truth of Jimmy's words, they couldn't believe that they had been truly saved and that a boy had given his life for their family after committing such an unpardonable sin against another. Why they had been spared they knew not, but forgiveness had been taught and blessings were now given in an abundance of gold and other riches which had once belonged to Anne.

The Athanatos Christian Ministries 2009

John Milton Award

goes to

Morgan Nystrom

Anzac, Alberta. Canada

Third Place

(Category: High School)

Bio: My name is Morgan Nystrom. I am eighteen years old and have recently graduated after being homeschooled all my life. Along with my seven siblings, of whom I am the oldest, I grew up in the city of Fort McMurray, Alberta. My family and I now reside in the small, rural community of Anzac, just south of Fort McMurray.

During my high-school years, I developed the ambition to write. My goal is to create wholesome novels that will inspire good character qualities in today's children and teenagers. My favourite writers include J.R.R Tolkien and L. M. Montgomery, who have both inspired me with their literary classics. I am currently enrolled with the Institute of Children's Literature and am in the process of writing my first children's novel.

GREATER LOVE

by Morgan Nystrom

Copyright 2009, All Rights Reserved

William Cabot rolled over in the dark and peered at the clock on the wall trying to see the time. He started as the old Grandfather clock in the hallway suddenly sent out four rolling chimes. William's wife shifted in bed beside him but did not wake. That old clock was loud but the entire family had been listening to it all their lives and hardly noticed it anymore.

The big man grunted as he swung his feet over the side of the bed. He walked slowly to the water jug and poured the water into the wash basin. Shivering, he splashed the icy water on his face and neck. Again, he glanced at the clock and reached for the towel, thinking that he had best hurry if they wanted to get the boat out by six.

William Cabot, who had inherited his last name from the Italian explorer John Cabot, was a fisherman. His father had been a fisherman and his grandfather had been a fisherman. William's son, William Cabot Jr., would no doubt also be a fisherman. The boy had already shown a keen interest in the trade. Many a time he had begged to be permitted to assist his father with his work. However, it was William Sr.'s opinion that his son should stay in school until he was fourteen years old. William had taken his son out in the sturdy fishing boat many times, but refused to allow his son to become part of the Cabot & Co. business until he had reached the respected age of fourteen.

Now the long awaited birthday had come and was, in fact, seven days past. William Cabot had finally hired his son as the newest addition to Cabot & Co. Fishing Business, and had promised that his son should accompany him the next time he was required to take the small fishing boat out for a fresh catch.

William pulled his clothes on over his long flannel underwear, for he knew, from years of experience, that a day out on the Atlantic Ocean was bound to be more than chilly. He looked out the bedroom window at the small town of St. John's, Newfoundland. The sky was still dark, but the faint tinge of orange on the horizon showed that the sun had begun to rise. He could hear the sound of waves breaking against the rocky shore and it reminded him to hurry.

Walking to the kitchen, William lit a lantern and set it on the table. Quickly he made a fresh pot of coffee and put it on the wood stove, then moved down the hallway to the boys' bedroom.

William and his wife had three sons: Erik was the youngest, only ten, and Lester, the next boy, was twelve. Then, of course, was the oldest son, William Jr. Friends and family had taken to calling the boy Jack so as not to confuse William Jr's name with his father's. No one knew how the name had originated, but it had stuck, and that was how he was known ever after. The room down the hall contained William's one and only daughter, Leslie, who had been named after her mother. Everyone who knew little Leslie called her "Papa's little girl" and "Papa" heartily agreed.

William pulled the quilt closer about the chins of his two younger sons. Even in the house, the morning air was chilly. He then moved to the bed of his oldest son.

Shaking the boy's shoulders, he whispered, "Jack, it's after four. You promised me you'd be up."

Jack rolled over and murmured sleepily, "Yes, father, I'll be along in a minute."

William chuckled to himself, knowing that if he left the room the boy would be fast asleep in less than a minute. He grabbed a corner of the warm quilt and whipped in back, exposing his son to the cold morning air.

Jack jerked himself up in bed. "Alright," he muttered, "I'm up."

"See that you are," replied the boy's father, laughing to himself. "When I was a boy my father used to douse me with cold water if I wasn't up on time."

Jack did not know whether to take this as a threat or not, but he washed and dressed himself hastily, resolving to rise at four o'clock sharp on future mornings. Today was the day of his first fishing trip as an official member of his father's business. He was very excited. For his birthday his father had given him all of his fishing gear and tackle. These were now in the fishing shed beside his father's gear. Jack was feeling very grown up and responsible. He was determined to show his father just how grown up and responsible he could be.

William and his son ate a swift breakfast, gathered the lunches that had been put together by Mrs. Cabot the night before, and were on their way. They did not bother to leave a note for Mrs. Cabot. As the wife of a fisherman, she was used to these early morning fishing trips.

Father and son walked briskly to the shore where they were met by William's three fishing partners. Quite a trio were these three men, for they differed greatly in every way. Jack had met these three men before but only briefly, therefore Mr. Cabot introduced them again.

"Jack," said William, placing his hand on the shoulder of a tall, skinny man in his early twenties whose slender build made him seem much taller than he really was. "This, as you may remember, is Lemuel Anderson."

Mr. Anderson reached out a hand to the boy saying, "Mornin' son, you just call me Lem."

Jack nodded as he took the man's outstretched hand. He thought that Lem moved like a puppet on strings and seemed to be all knees and elbows.

William turned to the next man who looked to be around sixty. He was leaning against a post with a cup of coffee in his hand. One look told Jack that this man was not a morning person.

"You remember John Buford, don't you, son?"

Jack nodded. "Good morning, sir," he said pleasantly.

Mr. Buford returned the boy's cheery greeting with a grunt and a nod, then went back to his coffee.

Lem, who was obviously a cheerful man who enjoyed his fun, jostled Mr. Buford playfully. "First impressions–especially in the mornin'–make Old John look like a crotchety old gentleman," he said to Jack. "You know, I've always said that–in the mornings–John is just like a shirt with too much starch in it: stiff, rattling and irritating." Lem laughed at his own joke, and once again jostled the old man, who muttered irritably under his breath and took another gulp of coffee. "But don't worry," the young man continued, "He'll soften up as the day goes on."

"Now, Jacky," said Lem, turning to the last man, "this is-," he stopped and cleared his throat dramatically, "James...Hayes." He pronounced each syllable of the man's name with almost painful precision.

If looks could kill Lemuel Anderson would not have had time for any last thoughts, for James Hayes shot him a look that would have withered any other man. Lem only laughed and rested his elbow on Jack's shoulder as he said, "Jim hates to be called by his full name. He says that his first and last name rhymes too much and makes him look foolish. I guess that shows you just how much schoolin' he's had."

Jack thought that he could understand how Mr. Hayes felt, for above all he absolutely detested to be called "Jacky".

Lem laughed again, "He would gladly strangle any one who dared introduce him as James. So," here Lem lowered his voice, "it'd probably be best if you just called him Jim."

Jack nodded and tried to look respectful as he shook Mr. Hayes hand and said, "Nice to meet you Mr. Ha-Jim."

Jim grunted and looked stern, but there was a twinkle in his eyes as he returned the boy's handshake.

"So, Cap'n," said Lem, addressing William, "shall we be starting then?"

When one looked at William and compared him to his companions, it became apparent just how big a man he was. His six foot five inch height brought him to almost a full head taller than any of the men, and his muscular build made him seem like a giant. He outweighed any one of the other men by nearly a hundred pounds and his obvious strength made his partners look small.

William turned to Lem, who was the youngest of the crew, with the exception of Jack, and said, "Yes, if we're ready, we can be on our way."

"Ay, ay, Cap'n," returned Lem energetically as he moved the fishing gear and food provisions to where the boat was resting on the rocky shore.

The three older men watched Lem and shook their heads. He could be ridiculous, but every one of them, even "Old John" and James Hayes, were fond of him.

After all of the gear and provisions were loaded, the men prepared to board. The sun was now well on its way up and William turned worried eyes to the sky which was becoming grey and overcast.

"Looks as though a storm is on its way, boys," he commented.

The other men looked up at the brooding sky.

"Ay, Cap'n," said Jim, "but by the look of things it won't hit before noon. We'll beat it."

"'Sides," cut in Lem, "we've toughed out storms afore."

In spite of the confidence of Jim and Lem, all four of the men knew that a storm on the Atlantic Ocean was nothing to take lightly. They also knew that the sea had claimed many lives and that it was a thing to be respected.

However, William and his men were experienced fishermen, and never before had a storm caught them unawares or off their guard.

So, having made the necessary preparations, the men shoved off and headed out to the open sea.

All three of William Cabot's partners enjoyed having young Jack aboard. It was a pleasure for them to have someone to whom they could show off. Even John Buford "softened up" just as Lem said he would.

The men enjoyed singing as they fished. A popular song in Newfoundland was "Saint Brendan's Voyage" and the five companions sang it lustily as they floated over the cold waters of the ocean.

Their catch consisted mainly of Cod, a great favorite among the Newfoundlanders. The average weight of a Cod fish is 10-25 pounds. Jim, however, boasted that he had once caught a 200 pound Cod.

Lem laughed heartily over this. "You never caught a *two hundred* pound Cod. I ain't never seen a Cod so big."

"Well, I think I've got a few more years under my belt than you, *youngster.*"

All the men enjoyed teasing Lem about his "tender age". They knew that he disliked having his age compared to theirs, and all laughed at the indignant look on his face when Jim referred to him as a "youngster".

"Did you know," asked John, turning to Jack, "that Cod can change color when they get to a certain depth in the ocean?"

Jack nodded. "Yes, they change from a reddish-brown to a grayish-green."

"Ay," said John, "but I prefer the reddish-brown ones. They look more appetizing."

John Buford must have been the only man in St. John's-the only man in Newfoundland for that matter-who was not fond of fish.

The men had become so preoccupied with their fishing that all of them, even William, had forgotten to watch the sky. Time passed more swiftly then they had expected, and suddenly, without warning, the storm was upon them.

It seemed as though the sky had fallen, and all the waters of the heavens came after it. The wind raged and moaned, and wave after wave beat relentlessly over the small fishing boat. The men clung desperately to the boat while William's huge form sheltered his son, keeping him from being washed overboard.

As time went by, the storm worsened. Suddenly, an enormous wave came over them like a giant carpet being rolled up and overturned their small fishing craft.

Gasping for breath, William rose to the surface. A wave crashed over him, forcing him under, and again he struggled to the surface. Treading water, he looked around frantically for Jack. Through the rain and the waves it was difficult to see anything, but then he caught a glimpse of his son struggling in the water. William swam toward the boy calling his name.

As he reached Jack he caught hold of his arm and dragged him through the water to where the overturned boat was tossing and rearing with the wind and the waves.

Lem and Jim were already there waiting for them.

"Where's John?" shouted William, struggling to be heard above the noise of the storm.

"I don't know," Lem shouted back, "I didn't see him come up...thought maybe he was with you."

"He may still be under the boat," Jim called.

A knot formed in William's stomach. "Jack, stay here and hold on," he ordered. "Jim, you too. Lem, you come with me."

Without a moment's hesitation both Lem and William released their hold on the boat and dove into the icy water.

The coldness of the water was like a punch in the chest as William swam under the boat. He had to stop himself from inhaling sharply. He pried his eyes open, but could see nothing in the dark water. His hands probed around the boat, but he could feel nothing but the hard wood beneath his fingers. There was no sign of John anywhere.

How long he was under the water for, William did not know, but it felt like hours. His lungs begged for air, and bubbles streamed from his mouth. It was not long before he was forced to return to the surface.

Grasping the boat tightly, he turned to his men. With a sudden shock, he saw Lem next to him. With one hand he was holding onto the boat, and with the other, he was holding onto John Buford. The old man was gasping for breath, and his limbs trembled violently as, with Lem's help, he held onto the overturned boat.

William heaved a sigh of relief and leaned his head against the boat. "Thank God," he breathed.

"I'll say," said Lem, laughing, "I really didn't want to go back under for you."

William shook his head. Even in a situation like this, Lem could still laugh.

After several hours, the storm still did not lessen and the waves washed over them threatening to loosen their tight hold on the boat. Then, William began to notice that the boat was much lower than it had been an hour ago. His end of the boat, especially, was so low in the water that only his head and shoulders were above the water. With a sudden tightening of his throat he realized that cracks had sprung in the boat. Water was seeping through. This greatly diminished the chance that the boat would simply float out the storm. The great weight of their bodies also added to the slow but steady sinking of the boat.

He said nothing to the men. What was there to say? There was no way to lessen the weight of the boat unless-

A sudden idea struck him. But no, he could not even think of it. He tried to push the thought away, but it kept nagging at him and refused to be forgotten. He knew that he accounted for most of the weight that was pulling the boat deeper and deeper into the water, dragging the men-his own son-to their deaths. But could he really do it? Could he really...*sacrifice himself* for the lives of his men?

He thought of his wife and three other children at home...waiting for him to return. He thought of how his children ran to the door, all talking at once, when he came home from a hard day's work. He thought of the smell of a home cooked meal and how they all joined hands as he said the blessing and thanked God for the continued health and protection of his family.

Then he looked at his son, Jack, holding onto the boat with both hands-his knuckles white with the effort, his lips blue with the cold, and his hair dripping water over his white face. Then, another thought came to William's mind.

Last night, before bed, he had read to the children from the Bible. One verse, short, simple, yet so effective. It was John 15:13, a verse that stood out in his mind so vividly that he could see it as clearly as if it had been etched into the wood of the boat. "Greater love hath no man than this, that a man lay down his life for his friends."

Greater love. That, thought William, must be the best kind of love. *Greater* love-the type of love you can't beat, that goes beyond any type of love one can think of.

Greater love.

Could he be capable of that kind of love? Could he lay down his life for his friends?

Again, he looked around. Lem was there next to him, still holding onto John, his hair plastered over his face. Then there was Jim, holding on tightly, trembling violently as a cold spell came over him. Last of all was Jack...his son. William sighed sadly. To think that his son's first real fishing trip should end like this.

Greater love, he thought again. After looking around once more at his companions he knew that he could indeed be capable of that kind of love.

Another wave washed over them, and the boat sunk treacherously low into the water. William turned to Lem. He was the youngest of his small crew, not counting Jack, but his natural cheerfulness and optimism made him the strongest of them all.

"Lem, look after the others," he said, so that only the young man could hear. "I need you to promise me that, no matter what, you'll see that their safe."

Lem looked confused. "What are you talking about, Cap'n?"

"Never mind, just promise. I'm leaving everything in your charge, do you understand?"

Lem did not understand, but he nodded, thinking that perhaps that cold was affecting his "Cap'n". He nodded reassuringly. "I promise Cap'n. Don't worry yourself on that account." Lem

turned back to John who was slipping slightly out of his grasp and helped him find a better hold on the overturned boat.

Another wave dashed against the small fishing craft. As it washed over, William released his hold on the boat and allowed himself to slip into the cold waters of the ocean.

Lem turned back to William Cabot's place as the boat immediately lightened and bounced back out of the water. His face whitened with shock when he saw that the Captain was gone.

"Cap'n", he yelled, scanning the tossing waters for a sign of his friend. "Cap'n Cabot!"

Lem's first instinct was to dive into the waters in search of the man, but he suddenly remembered his promise and knew that he must stay.

The other men, realizing what had happened, took up the call. But there was no answer, nor any sign of the Captain's body. Jack rested his head on the boat which floated much higher now that it was relieved of William's great weight. He was weeping, his tears mingling with the rain.

Lem looked around at the small crew that was now in his charge, and thought about what his Captain had been trying to tell him a moment before. Lem chided himself severely. He should have known that the man had been up to something. Oh, it was so like him to...Lem could not think of it and, like Jack, he leaned his head against the side of the boat and wept.

Barely an hour later the storm subsided, and half an hour after that, a rescue boat was sighted.

The men were picked up and given blankets to warm themselves as best they could until they reached land. They searched the waters briefly for the body of William Cabot but, knowing that there was no hope for him and that it was more important to get the others back to land and hospital care, they headed for the St. John's port.

Once they had landed, Lem stopped only long enough to get himself a dry pair of clothes. After that he headed at once to tell Mrs. Cabot the sad news.

He did not bother to knock as he reached the house, but opened the door quietly and stepped in. He looked around and saw no one.

Suddenly his eyes fell upon something that again brought the tears to his eyes.

William Cabot's Bible.

Lem had seen the Captain with this book so many times that it seemed almost a part of him. He picked it up reverently, and opened it to a place that William had marked with a short strand of ribbon. Immediately he noticed a short passage that had been underlined in red. The tears overflowed and streamed down Lem's cheeks as he read it.

"Greater love hath no man than this, that a man lay down his life for his friends."

The End

The Athanatos Christian Ministries 2009

William Blake Award

goes to

Nate Rankin

Richardson, TX

Third Place

(category: High School)

Bio: My name is Nate Rankin and I am the Loudest and Proudest member of the Fightin' Texas Aggie Class of 2013. My home is in Richardson but in the fall I will go to school to Texas A&M. Growing up I was fascinated with the fantastical worlds of J.R.R. Tolkien and C.S. Lewis. I had read The Lord of the Rings and The Chronicles of Narnia by the time I completed 6th grade. My Mom is an English teacher and was the one who inspired me to pick up books. My dad was the one who inspired ambition and told me I could be anything I wanted to be. The story was inspired by Josh Hamilton and Craig Ferguson and their struggles with addiciton and alcoholism. My main writing inspiration was Douglas Coupland as well as Craig Ferguson.

To Make A Wretch His Treasure

By Nate Rankin

Copyright 2009, All Rights Reserved

How deep the Father's love for us,
How vast beyond all measure
That He should give His only Son
To make a wretch His treasure
How great the pain of searing loss,
The Father turns His face away
As wounds which mar the chosen One,
Bring many sons to glory
Behold the Man upon a cross,
My sin upon His shoulders

> *Ashamed I hear my mocking voice,*
> *Call out among the scoffers*
> *It was my sin that held Him there*
> *Until it was accomplished*
> *His dying breath has brought me life*
> *I know that it is finished*
> *I will not boast in anything*
> *No gifts, no power, no wisdom*
> *But I will boast in Jesus Christ*
> *His death and resurrection*
> *Why should I gain from His reward?*
> *I cannot give an answer*
> *But this I know with all my heart*
> *His wounds have paid my ransom*
> -Stuart Townend

For the man who has lost hope but not his chance, for those who seek the heavenly kingdom and find a corrupt world, for those who suffer in the name of our Lord yet continue to bear their crosses, may you find encouragement in these words...

"My name is Tucker Collins. And I am an alcoholic. I've been sober for six weeks now, but I have wasted away the last three years. Now, in contrast to a lot of you in my situation, I wasn't abused as a child, my daddy never drank, and my momma was around when I was a kid. They were there, and they were good to me. I went to private schools my whole life, went to church every Sunday, and I was baptized before I could read. I guess what I'm getting at is — or trying to say to you is — that I –I — don't know why I am the way that I am. I don't know who set me off or what caused me to suddenly start binge drinking on the weekends, showing up to church hungover, announcing to the whole congregation that Jesus was outside on the street corner holding up a crude cardboard sign that wrote some wretched message to the world of how it would end." I paused at that moment and looked up at the rest of the group in the poorly lit gymnasium and unclenched my suddenly sweaty palms from the podium. I took a deep breath. "I am Tucker Collins. And I am an alcoholic."

"Hi Tucker," the crowd responded. It was a dull murmur, and I knew that a good majority of the people were not interested in my story at all because they had one of their own self-therapeutic speeches to give. And after all who would pay attention to a tale told by an idiot when you had your own to give? So I walked back to the back of the crowd where my seat was, sat down, and tried to compress my body to conform to the chair as much as possible.

Slowly the rest of the group got up to the front and talked about their progressions or digressions and triggers and suppressants. It would end with Chris thanking everyone and congratulating people on the progress they had made and how this really worked and blah blah blah.

I don't suppose I despised Chris; I suppose I just felt mad at him because while I was now sober I couldn't get past the fact that I didn't know the reasons for my regressions. As I had told the mass, I didn't know why I started. I wanted more results than the weekly circle time support groups and the two minutes of confession to the crowd. I wanted a cure for the flu and all I was getting was medicine for the symptoms.

Of course I need to explain myself further. This was not the first time I had been sober. I suppose the first eighteen years should count, but my first attempt to quit ended up failing after weekly sessions like these. I stringed together about four months before I relapsed. That following morning I awoke in a stranger's house soaked in a mixture of beer, vodka, pool water, and the stench of what I can best guess was my own urine. It was a Sunday, so I dared not go to church, and I sat in my car drifting between sleep and blackouts. The following Tuesday I still felt sick, though I gathered it was more from guilt then from the alcohol and skipped the AA meeting. That was my first relapse.

When I told my parents a month ago that I was sober again, they cringed. But I was past what they thought. Three relapses can make even the most honest parents question themselves. But I never blamed them. Sure I blamed my Scottish heritage, claiming it was in my blood, and I blamed peer pressure, and I rationalized it to a point where I could convince people that Christ himself was an alcoholic. But never my parents. I knew they didn't believe me any more than Bill Maher believes in a god, but I had a new inspiration. Her name was Sarah.

It was a cloudy morning. The wind blew through the trees and whistled in the gutters. It carried the tiny wet messengers of rain to the ground, declaring it was time for growth and a new beginning. As the drops hit my face, I began to look up. I could see the hope of light through the clouds. Even when it's cloudy you can always see the sun.

Feeling as if pencils were pushing my eyes back into my sockets, I got up. I observed the house whose porch I had used for a bed. Mixed red brick with a green door. I rang the doorbell. Sully answered and I grunted a hello. It was still early. Around seven I believe. So I crept carefully over the empty beer cans, the kegs, the passed out human beings, and their personal belongings.

I grabbed my keys, wallet, and phone. They would be my lifelines now. Change was calling, and I would need a way to answer, pay and get to it. Sully said something about not driving, but I flipped him off and was on my way out. There was change to be made and it wasn't going to be stopped by some Mick who was no doubt intelligently inferior and more hungover than I was.

My first stop was coffee. The myth is that coffee will soak up the alcohol and allow you to have your wits more about you. Whoever created the myth was obviously never above the legal alcohol-driving limit. It doesn't matter what you put in your body if the alcohol's already there. The best thing coffee can do is caffeinate you. I ordered black coffee and mixed it with some crème I seemed to perpetually have in my car. I sipped it slowly as I stared at my three new lifelines.

I had no apartment as I had decided I wasn't going to come up with the money anyway and had left early. I had no relatives within a good 200 miles of myself. And all my friends were hungover or not talking to me. I listed off my options, which took all of five seconds. I could go to rehab again or I could find a decently sober friend and crash with him until I made a decision. At about this time I noticed that all twenty tables in the café had been filled up. Then along came Sarah.

Of all the tables in the café, of all the coffee shops around the city, of all the people she could have sat with, she asked me. Don't ask me why. I'm sure my eyes were still bloodshot and that I had the hangover stubble on my chin, but she was polite and had a smile on her face and asked if she could sit. I said she could and she asked why I was staring at my things. "They're my friends." I said half-humorously.

She smiled and said, "Do they have names?"

"Phone, wallet, and keys" which I expected to kill the conversation, but she kept going.

"How bout Ringy, Money, and Shiny."

"So my keys can only shine is that it?"

" They're not driving right now and the sun just came out, I can see the money in your wallet, and your phone's going off." She said with a smile. I looked down and noticed she was right. It was just my alarm clock. I turned it off and muttered a "thanks."

"So I haven't seen you around here before. You new?"

" To town or coffee?" This made her laugh. It sounded like music. I caught myself.

" I mean this isn't a place that gets a lot of new customers. Kind of a hole in the wall." A pause. "Not a usual customer I suspect."

"Uh no. Not here." I wanted to say more. I really did, but I was so tired and so distressed. I just took a sip of my coffee and sighed.

Heavily.

"You okay?" she asked.

"I've been better," I said as I scratched my chin. She just looked at me sympathetically. "I need to use the bathroom, 'scuse me."

I didn't stay in the bathroom long. Just long enough to wash my face and say a little prayer. I've always wondered why God doesn't talk back. Maybe the whole religion thing was a farce. Maybe God had filled up heaven and was just mocking those of us still holding out hope. Maybe after we didn't give him any room in the inn he wouldn't give us any. Seemed logical to me at the time.

I came back and was surprised that Sarah was still there. What she said next blew my brain. "Finnegan Tucker Collins you're coming with, and I'm going to help you" I had left my lifelines on the table. Still I tried to play stupid.

"Help me? Whaddya mean?"

"Come on, you have four dollars in your wallet, you obviously don't have a house key, and your background on your phone is you holding up a Bud Light bottle looking completely wasted."

"To be fair that's dip-spit so you can't assume I'm an alcoholic. And call me Tucker"

"I didn't say you were an alcoholic."

"You implied."

"Please let me help you," She was begging now. And as much as the fiber of my muscles twitched and the core of me despised her nosiness and despised her for wanting to help me, I broke. There were no words; I just took her hand and she led me.

We ended up talking for an hour in the parking lot. I was awkward at best with her. It's funny how the booze will get you feeling loose. It shakes off the nerves. Plus you can be brutally honest with people and not even realize it. But there I was dancing around with my mouth trying to recapture the intellect I used to have. And the thing was . . . it was wonderful. Being in an awkward conversation was something I hadn't participated in since high school. I was re-learning my innocence that had been paralyzed by the alcohol. I managed to get her number, which she of course wrote on the back of a business card for an AA group. Did I mention she wanted to help?

So six weeks later there I was trying to find the cure for the itch. I walked out of the doors of the safe haven into the depraved crooked world. It's hard to believe that architects are still building everything straight. I hopped in my car and drove myself to Sarah's. I had been staying with her since I told her my parents didn't want me back. I had lied. One vice for another I suppose, but she made me feel safe. And it's not like we were sleeping together. I don't even know if we were in a relationship. I just couldn't stand the world anymore.

"We're like the air" Sully use to say. "Our days are like a fleeting shadow." Took me a couple years to figure out he got that from the Bible. Told me that was the reason we should drink up today and barf out tomorrow. So there we all would be . . . drinking until our vision was blurry and fighting each other over how many beers we thought we had in us. And I have to say it was great. That was before my guilt, and before I thought I had a problem. It was as if being an alcoholic took some invincibility out of me. I now had a problem, and no one wants to befriend a problem because no one wants to fix something that could be wrong. Then you just realize that there actually is something wrong with you. It's the same reason those self-conscious-adolescent-oh-my-gosh-will-I-ever-get-a-boyfriend-girls don't look in the mirror. They don't want to see flaws because they're too embarrassed to fix them. And the ones that do aren't satisfied and end up with a problem. The whole healthy self-esteem concept is a load of crap. People hate flaws so we cover them with booze, makeup, a smile, or any number of lies and deceptions.

When I got home, as it were, Sarah wasn't there. Funny, she hadn't said anything. So I made myself a pizza and watched Comedy Central. After I finished, I tried her cell phone. It must have been off because it went straight to voicemail. I threw my phone on the couch and mulled over my current situation.

I thought about Sarah. She was about five and a half feet tall. Light skin but not fair, dark hair but not black and straight. She had really warm brown eyes. The kind of eyes that talk like angels. She had a cute nose that was very round like a miniature golf ball. You could call her physically attractive, but she never wore makeup except a little eyeliner, and she almost always wore a t-shirt with blue jeans. She didn't have an accent, which was refreshing. It reminded me of home. She was one of those girls that was attractive because of her heart. I could have always gone and lived with Sully, but I could have also always put a gun to my head. Sarah gave me a pillow for my head and an escape from the bedlam. She laughed at my jokes and would tell me she loved me for them. We both had moved past the awkward parking lot stage and had moved towards the help-a-fellow-Christian-out-stage. As an only child I never knew what a sibling was like. This was close, probably even better. I still didn't know what her mission was. She just told me it was God's will. "But why not go pick up some homeless bum on the street and help him?" I asked one day.

"Because he won't appreciate it the way you will. You haven't realized how much better you are than this, Tuck."

"Than what?" I asked

"Than everything." And she stopped at that. I didn't care I just wanted to get sober and back to church on Sundays. She was very adamant about church. And who could blame her with the pastor there. He was so human. Every other pastor I knew was an old guy who had that holier-than-thou attitude, despite any rebuking towards it. Pastor Jake would always get up there and be an inspirational eeyore. Talking about everything he sucked at and every little doubt he had. It was as if the sky was falling, and God was burying us underground to avoid the impact. The gist I got from him was this, we will sin everyday and God will take us back. And then we'll sin some more and God will take us back. And then we'll spit on his face, drive nails in his arms and legs, whip him to the brink of death, insult him, deny him, and curse his very creation, and he will still take us back.

When Sarah hadn't gotten home by ten, I started to worry. She always kept tabs on me. Always called me and left me encouraging texts. I called again. Voicemail again. I jumped up and looked for her phonebook. I called around to close friends of hers I had met. No one had seen or heard from her. I began to really freak out. It was worse than the time I had done mushrooms with my friends in college. I called again. Nothing. I needed her now. I barely knew her, yet I was dependent on her grace. I finally realized I wasn't going to contact her. So I tried to think of something that would calm me down. So naturally I went and bought some alcohol.

Thirty minutes later I was back at Sarah's house with a bottle of Grey Goose, some Southern Comfort, and a six-pack of Budweiser. I had to have stared at it for thirty minutes before I decided what I would do. I was half hoping Sarah would walk in and freak out at the alcohol eighteen inches away from me. But no luck. It was just the booze and me. No one would have to know. I could drink any one of them then return the others and fall asleep on the couch, with little to no hangover at all.

But then I thought of Sarah. I couldn't do it to her. So I went to her room and pulled out her Macbook and started typing. The sun had just come up.

I called Sarah's friend Cherry. She said she hadn't seen or heard from her since the day before she disappeared. I still have the three things of alcohol stashed away. But I'm convincing myself they're for celebration when she comes home.

But why did she leave? I heard my mom one time talking about how some people who did kindly things were angels sent from heaven. I wondered if Sarah was some fantastical angelic body, whose presence I had just been completely ignorant of this whole time. Maybe she was in deep with the mob, and they finally found her. Maybe she didn't really own this house and some realtor would walk in any moment and announce it was for sale by the bank and that I would have to leave. I didn't know. I was looking for clues but nothing turned up. She was neat. Didn't have more than two drawers of clothes, nothing hidden in her closets, no safes, no weird phone messages, nothing.

I thought back to the parable of the lost sheep. Sheep gets lost, master leaves the whole herd behind, and comes back with the lamb no problem. But this seemed the total opposite. When was the last time the master got lost? She wasn't supposed to get lost. She was supposed to have found me and fixed me, and then I could go back home and get a decent job and earn a decent living. But here I was alone. Staving off my itch for alcohol with a Monster energy drink. There was only one weird incidence with Sarah that I can remember. We were on a quasi-date—as I said I don't know if we ever had a boyfriend-girlfriend relationship before—at a somewhat fancy restaurant. I was holding her hand, and we were having a really deep conversation—and by deep conversation I mean I was straight up flirting with her. She looked really deep into my eyes and she got the biggest little smile anyone's seen this side of the Atlantic. All of a sudden I see this big brawny looking guy walk in with a girl so beautiful it made me want to crawl on my belly like a reptile. Since Sarah was facing away, she didn't see him at first. Then he looked our way and did a double take at both of us. At the same instant she saw him and breathed out the only curse word I'd ever heard her say. "Let's get the check. Now," she said immediately after.

"You know that guy over there?"

"I think I see our waiter."

"Hey!" I snapped my fingers in her face. "You know him?"

There was a long pause. "No"

"You can just say you don't want to talk about it."

"I don't know him Tuck." She turned to our waiter and asked him for the check.

And that was it. There wasn't anything else really peculiar about her. I had met a handful of her friends, Cherry being her closest, and they were all a lot like her. They all were sympathetic to me and wanted to help me through my "trials". After wandering around the apartment for another hour, I decided to call Cherry again. This time I was going to ask about the guy.

"Hello?" she said after picking up after the fourth ring.

"Cherry it's Tucker; I need to ask you something."

"What's up hon?"

"Did Sarah ever have a relationship with anyone that might have been bad in any way?" I was sounding very vague, but I guess I didn't want to leave anything out. Anything important, I needed to hear.

"Well—oh—there was this really serious boyfriend—some Irish guy can't really remember his name—she dated a little more than a year ago. Why?"

"What did he look like?"

"Uh—about—six twoish, really broad, red hair…" I didn't listen to the rest because I knew whom she was talking about. Suddenly I felt like I was falling. I felt like someone had tossed me out of the sky and I was part of this big puzzle that was cascading down headed for a hard fall of realization. But I needed more clues. I hung up, grabbed my keys and an energy drink, and was in my car before Cherry called back. My mind was racing. She knew him! Why did she lie? There was something there that I needed to know, something dark and repressible. I needed a name.

My first stop was the restaurant we had eaten at, Hillenshire's. Somehow he had to be known by someone there. He had made heads turn around the whole room. On the ride there my head was starting to feel light. My hands were getting clammy. At this point I usually required a stiff drink and a round of beer pong. But I kept calm. As best I could at the least. I tried breathing through my nose. Slowly. Catching my wind and wits about me, I turned into the parking lot.

It was the middle of the afternoon, a little before 4:00, so no one was going to be there most likely. I opened the door and shivered. They had the air conditioning on full blast in there. I walked up to the hostess as she greeted me.

"How often do you normally work here?" I asked.

She was a bit taken aback and then she smiled and said, "I work full time here, mostly in the evenings."

Before she could ask or say anything further I came back, "So you would recognize a normal customer?"

"Yes, ah you looking for someone in particular? Maybe they got a reservation."

"Um—is there a—well I was here once and um—is there a tall red-headed guy, probably comes in with a hot date?"

"Honey, we're in South Bahston, they're a lotta guys that look like dat, and frankly I don't know what you would define as a hot date." She was getting a bit of an attitude on herself.

"I mean like model type. He really stands out—like a lot of people recognize him…"

"You might be talking about Peter McCreedy, the manager's son."

"How often is he here?"

"He's probably over at his bar right now. Three blocks down, take a right outta here and just drive. It's on the right." She said the name of it, but I couldn't hear it. I had to find this Peter guy. Maybe he would know something about Sarah I didn't. It would likely be awkward, but I had to know. I never knew when it would be too late.

I walked into the bar and asked for the manager. The bartender said he wasn't in, so I asked where he was.

"Prolly on a hot date. Why? Who's asking? I ain't never seen you in here before."

"Did he used to have a girlfriend named Sarah!"

At the sound of that the guy's eyes bugged out and his eyebrows rose. His forehead muscles tightened and his mouth shrunk to the size of his thumbnail.

"Hey, if you know somethin 'bout Sarah you better keep yuh mouth shut. It's a sore subject around here." He looked at me suspiciously yet inquisitively. "Yon't look like her type. Why doncha sit down, loosen up."

"I'm an alcoholic. I didn't come here for booze." I stopped and glared at him to make sure he got the message I wasn't having anything. "What happened with Sarah and Peter?"

"You sure you don't want a drink?"

I glared.

"Fine, I'll getchu a water, because it's a long story." He set the bottle down and started talking. "So Petey comes in one day and tells me he's got a new girl. I shrug it off, cuz whaddo I care, you know? He tells me about her and starts talking about how she's changed him and how he's going back to church. Well not real church, da Proddy kind. Anyway he starts talking about how he thinks we're doing the wrong thing here. Selling alcohol and how its leadin' to all this sin and makin' people screwed up you know. Course he never goes troo wid it, because a bar in Boston is like a baseball field in Iowa. If you build it, they will come. Anyways about nine months in he's starting to get really depressed, and he's mopin' around here like a dog widout a bone. I ask him what's wrong, and he says that he asked Sarah to marry him and she said no. The gall! Anyway I tell him to go find a new girl, but he says he don't want another girl, he wants this one. Come to find out, she won't marry him cuz a da bar. I tell him I'll run the bar and he can go marry her. Well he wouldn't have it. Says I'm trying to steal his business, which I kinda am, and he steams on outta here. Next thing I hear she's been in bed wid his best friend this whole time. Now I ain't sayin' nothing here, but two weeks later cops call Petey telling him this same guy's body was found dead in his apartment. Says it looks like a mob job. Now you didn't hear it from me, but someone called Sarah and told her to skip town and lie low. Since then, see no, hear no, speak no, know what I'm saying?" He winked.

I was sick. Physically. It was worse than any binge-drinking hangover I had ever had. The room started to spin. I hadn't had a sip of anything, not even the bottled water. My hands were wet and every cell on my body felt like it had a heartbeat of its own. I gave the guy a tip, Sonny, he asks me to call him, and I head for the door.

Suddenly here it was right before me. My idol, my savior was in all reality probably dead or being hunted. I had called the police and filed a missing persons report, but nothing had shown up this last week. I didn't have much time. I had to find her. The only way to do that though was confront McCreedy. I couldn't speak his first name since the conversation at the bar. This much I knew, though, if Sarah had been killed, I could go right to the police and get McCreedy in handcuffs really quick. If not, then she had probably escaped again and wasn't going to come back to Boston any time soon. I had to act. I wasn't going to be able to pay any bills of hers, so I had to form a plan.

I wound up calling the police. I talked to a cop that said he would hook me up with a wire and have me see if I could get anything on the murder of McCreedy's former friend or of Sarah since it was still an open case. I prayed for the former and against the latter. Basically my plan was to go to McCreedy's bar, find a way to not invoke a fight, and get out of there with something incriminating. I'd have to lull him into it, though. I couldn't come on too strong or too eager. "God have mercy on me," I prayed.

A bar fight is a lot different sober than it is the right way. I tried to play it cool. But it got out of hand fast, and before I knew it the Scots were fighting the Irish again. You'd think we'd learn. Anyway I walked in and noticed he was serving drinks. It was a Tuesday, not a lot of business that night. I went up to him and asked for a coffee with some cream.

"You know there's a Starbucks right down the road don't ya?"

"Yeah—just—I don't like Starbucks."

"You been in here before?"

" Uh no not really."

"I recognize ya, it's like déjà vu all over again."

"I know whatcha mean. Hey is that a wedding ring?"

"It's a family ring." He added. "I don't believe in marriage."

I sipped my coffee and said, "Is that cuz of Sarah?"

Now let me take the time in telling you I got a 1300 on my SAT, I maintained a 3.5 in high school, and before I dropped out of college I was passing every class. But despite all of those numbers, I could still be stupid. Blame it on the emotion of the situation, blame it on the fact that I'm bad with conversation, blame it on the alcohol that had given me plenty of practice through the years. Blame it on anything you want, but when I saw the vein in that stupid Mick's head, I knew I had hit a nerve with the force of a .50 caliber bullet.

He lowered his voice almost to a whisper, "And who told you about Sarah?" he said through gritted teeth.

"Just tell me where she is okay." I said calmly but spewing anxiety.

"That whore left town right after her boyfriend got killed." I could see his mouth twitch like he was happy.

"And who killed him?"

"I think we gotta troublemaker in here." He shouted in a raised voice.

"Just tell me where she is, I know you did something to her." I yelled back. This got the entire place's attention.

"Yeah? She didn't stick around long enough to get what was comin!"

"And what was that?"

"Here you can pass it on to her when you see her in hell!" He rolled up his sleeves and lunged at me. I spilled my coffee on his eyes and we grappled on the ground. Before I could hit him, my fists were being held by two other drunks, and I was being tackled by a third. I was on the ground with four guys on me trying to suffocate me. Then I managed to grab one guy's arm and bite it. He screamed, and I jabbed at his teeth, which fell like a rock climber without a rope. I started kicking and moving my legs, while simultaneously head locking the guy with no front teeth. I got another fist free and crashed them both like symbols on McCreedy's head. I elbowed Toothy for good measure and then spun out of the mob's grip. I grabbed a shot glass and slammed it against thug number two's forehead, who looked a little like my dad. Pops screamed and I lunged and tackled him. I got on my knees and held his throat as I delivered a knockout punch. At the instant I turned around, thug number three avalanched on top of me. Of all the guys he slobbered the most. So Spitty got one in the family jewels and then got a crown on his head from my now broken hand. Finally there was Petey.

We exchanged bruises until I finally got him in a nelson. I slammed his head against a table and screamed. "What did you do with her?! Who did you send after her?!"

"If the guys I sent after her had found her, she'd have been on the news by now! But hey, be patient, I'm sure she'll turn up." He mocked cruelly. At that moment cops came rushing in and hit us both. I was knocked out before I heard the siren.

I woke up in a holding cell. Apparently I'm too good of a fighter. When a bald cop saw me awake, he called out for some guy named Pickles. Or maybe it was Piggles. I couldn't tell. Everything was blurry like a snowstorm without the snow. And it was hot. Pickles unlocked the cell and told me to come with him. He kind of looked like an albino pickle. We sat down and about fifteen minutes later I was aware enough to tell him my story.

"I don't know if we can get charges on him. Depends if he talks anymore. But we might be able to look into the murder of the last guy. You never know. Funny thing, though, turns out the guy was gay that got murdered. So either he had the wrong hit or she was never cheating on him."

"Allegedly?" I smirked

"Allegedly." He smiled. "You're free to go; no charges are being pressed by us or by the owner because, well, he's kinda busy as you can imagine. We'll look into your missing person. Maybe if we get this to the media she'll see it and come out of hiding."

I smiled. I knew she wasn't coming out of hiding. I wasn't planning on even going back to her house. Somehow I knew that the false accusation against her and her affair would reveal itself. She was too good for that. I walked out of that station proud of myself. I had been alcohol free for almost two months now and going strong. I was back on the narrow road between the ravines that were waiting to receive me when I relapsed. But I had regained my balance and was walking tall. And as the sunlight hit me, and spackled the dried blood on my lips and eyebrows, and screamed into my pupils, I felt something for the first time. I felt loved. I felt loved by God as if he himself had pulled me out of that mob and embraced me like a mother with her newborn baby.

It's strange. This whole experience of losing Sarah has made me realize something. It's not her I've been searching the streets for. It's been Jesus. It's been both of them. The day will come when I see her again, smiling, with open arms. Until then I'll search madly. I will ransack the town looking for my savior. I will bellow their name and cry out to them for strength. I will scream to the skies to lead me to her. And when that day comes and I do find her, something miraculous and fantastical will occur that this world has not seen. Hell will freeze over and the volcanoes will spew ice and snow proclaiming the devil has been defeated. Thieves will come off of their crosses, households will be divided, investors will leave Wall Street, mob bosses will confess to the cops, the cancerous will be healed, dictators will hand over their power to their people, the very foundations of mankind will be destroyed because they are rooted in sin, and they will all join me in my rejoicing. We will all crowd the streets with mad dancing and praises that deafen the most wicked of deeds, and I will knock on every door of every house and I will proclaim, "I have found my Savior! I have found the one who believed in me when I was buried beneath my sin and pulled me out of my own self-loathing. And even in my darkest hour when the weight of my sins fell upon me and I thought he was not there, I fought ravenously as he pulled me towards him. And as the fighting got tougher, he shielded me from the dangers of the world and sacrificed himself so that I might find him, and Behold I have found him." And I have. I, a wretched, heartbroken, desolate, barren wasteland of a human being have found the treasure that gives me everlasting life. Why has this happened? Because of Love. This existential happening came into being because one day the Creator of every microorganism, of every living thing, of every star, of every galaxy sent his son to take my place.

I will find Sarah. I will find her as surely as God has found me.

The 2009 Sojourner Leatherwork

Flannery O'Connor Award

Goes to Josèphe-Anne Rocke

Port-of-Spain, Trinidad & Tobago

Third Place

(Category: High School)

Bio: Born in the Republic of Trinidad & Tobago, Josèphe-Anne has had a passion for writing since she was 11-years-old. In addition to fiction, she also enjoys composing poetry.

Now 18, her hobbies include drawing, figure skating, and studying nature and mythology. She is currently at work on her first novel.

SECRETS OF THE PHOENIX

Josèphe-Anne Rocke

Copyright 2009, All Rights Reserved

Long ago, it was once said that a magnificent, gold-plumed phoenix protected the Gem Kingdom. His name was Milcham.

Very few had actually seen Milcham. But most of those who had seen him said that he had promised them a priceless gift.

In ancient times – before the Gem Kingdom even existed – Milcham vanquished the one known as the Ultimate Evil. He is usually referred to as Demogorgon; his influences were – and still are – quite strong. Yet, Milcham is stronger.

Demogorgon assumes many different forms, and he shuns all things good and happy. However, if Milcham is called on by name, the wicked one flees immediately.

One day, Milcham suddenly vanished. No one knew what happened to him or where he was.

Years passed since his mysterious disappearance. Eventually people lost hope and faith, until the point where many from the younger generations thought that the story of the golden phoenix was merely a myth.

* * *

The cave was dark and eerie, filled with nothing but a chilling silence. And then, the monster appeared – it's horrid, bloodshot eyes piercing through the blackness. It's bumpy, sallow face twisted into a terrible grin as it plucked the bird's feathers out, one by one.

Tears rolled down the victim's face while he cried out in agony...

At that moment the boy awakened, with the sound of malicious laughter still ringing in his ears. Shrugging off the effects of his nightmare, Daniel headed straight downstairs to his father's room. Inside, he found his sister already spoon feeding the sickly, old man.

For the past two years, the aging man had been bedridden with an incurable disease. Daniel's mother had died shortly after giving birth to him, so his older sister, Miriam had been the only maternal influence in his life.

Ever since Dad had taken ill, young Daniel had been forced to find employment, just as Miriam was obliged to stay at home and care for the invalid.

Right now, the boy stood in the doorway observing the ever monotonous scene. It took a while before Miriam noticed he was there. "Good morning, Dan." she said, as the shut-in lifted his head slightly. "Did you sleep well?" she asked.

"Actually," Daniel replied, "I didn't."

"Why is that?"

"I had a dream, last night." he told them.

Miriam looked a bit concerned. "What sort of dream?" she questioned.

"The bad sort." Daniel began to recall the horror he had experienced during his restless slumber. "I dreamt that Milcham was being plucked alive. He was pleading for someone to help him." he explained.

At this, his father gasped and nearly choked on his porridge. Miriam just stared from one to the other with eyes wide open.

"Do you know what this means, my son?" the ill man coughed out the words.

"No." Dan replied in all honesty.

"It must have been a vision, Daniel. Don't you see? No one knows what ever happened to Milcham, and now you see in your dream that he is in great danger."

The two siblings had no idea what their father was getting at, and so Miriam enquired, "What do you think we should do about it?"

All that their father said was, "That phoenix is the noblest creature in the universe. To be of any assistance to him would be a great honor indeed."

Later that day, while Dan was toiling in Mr. Flint's smithy, those very words echoed at the back of his mind. The young man was employed as the blacksmith's apprentice.

Just as the boy was hammering out a sheet of stainless steel, someone entered the shop. It was "Pompous Percy," Percival Quartz, who had recently been elevated to the rank of general. Dan tried to ignore him and pretend he wasn't there, but it was no use.

Percival strutted straight up to Dan's work table and demanded with the utmost authority, "Where is your master?"

Without looking up, Dan replied, "I'm afraid he isn't here."

"I see." commented the general. "I just popped in to check on my new shield."

"We're up to our necks in special orders, Percival."

"It's *General Quartz* to commoners like you, Daniel." Percy intoned. "Anyway, I take it that you haven't finished it, as yet?"

Dan did not answer, but glued his eyes to the work in front of him.

Percy made to leave, then paused at the doorway, "Oh right," he began, "I meant to ask you – Haven't you tried registering for the king's army, again?" he jeered. "I swear you've put on an ounce since last year."

"Just get out of here, Percy! Your order will be ready by the end of the month!" the apprentice growled.

Percival shot him a self-satisfied smirk before departing on his black stallion, Obsidian.

Daniel loathed every second he spent in Percy's presence, for their sour relationship went back a long way.

The decorated commander had begun life as a lowly peasant right here, in the village of Beryllium. The boy himself was barely a year older than Daniel, but had always been rather large for his age.

At the barely eligible age of thirteen, Percival Quartz became the youngest military recruit in the kingdom's history. And mere months ago, he also became the youngest army general on record.

Poor Dan had been trying to make the cut for the past four years in a row. Each time, he had come home disappointed. He always aced the mental exams, but he continuously failed the weight requirement.

A lanky, string bean of a boy was Daniel. No matter how hard he tried to gain weight, he was doomed to be a runt forever, it seemed. And Percy's favorite pastime was pointing out this fact.

That night, Dan was troubled by the same dream of Milcham and the troll. This time, it seemed even worse than before. He could almost smell the monster's putrid breath, feel the bird's pain... Then suddenly, he was jolted back to reality.

Unable to go back to sleep, he wandered out of his bedroom and into the kitchen. And to his surprise, he found his sister already there. She too, had been unable to rest.

He explained to her how exasperated he was. Dan was not sure what he believed at this point, but he knew he couldn't continue being an insomniac.

"King Feldspar is a faithful believer in Milcham. I'm sure he'd be willing to help." Miriam suggested.

* * *

Clad in nothing but his peasant rags, the boy felt completely out-of-place as he entered the king's elaborate throne room.

Seated in his lofty perch, the king addressed him in empowering bass tones. "What is your name, young man?"

Dan dared to look up at the royal – a tall, burly man in his early 50s, covered in furs and velvet. But it wasn't the king's appearance that shocked him.

Standing right beside the ruler's seat was none other than Percival Quartz. *Why did he have to be here?* Daniel wondered.

Percy was staring directly at him; their eyes locked for an instant. Yet, the apprentice managed to compose himself, and answer the king, saying, "I am Daniel Garnet, son of Jonah Garnet, Your Highness."

"Well then, Daniel, why have you come to see me, today?" Feldspar enquired.

Daniel took a deep breath. "I believe I know where Milcham is." he stated.

This news obviously roused the king's curiosity, because he leaned forward in his seat slightly.

Dan felt obliged to continue. "For the past few days, I've been having visions of a cave in the Jade Mountains. I believe that

Milcham has been kidnapped, and is being held there by a troll."

With a toss of his bouncy, blonde locks, Percival spoke, "My King, surely we cannot trust the word of a mere peasant boy!" he sneered. "I mean, how do we know he isn't lying?"

Daniel stood up, dumfounded by Percy's accusations.

"May I remind you, Percival, that you once lived as he does." Feldspar said to Percy, who humbled at once. Turning to Daniel now, he said, "However, my general has raised a valid point. Times are too uncertain for me to send even a handful of my men to accompany you, especially with the mysterious disappearance of so many of my horses.

Nonetheless, I am willing to commission you, Daniel Garnet, to do everything in your power to find Milcham. Therefore, I give you this," he removed the pendant from around his neck and handed it to the young apprentice, "so that everywhere you go, people will know that you are on a quest for me."

Feldspar then signaled a servant. "See to it that Mr. Garnet is given all the supplies he needs."

When he returned home, Miriam and Dad were pleased to hear that the king was in support of Daniel's mission. Dan himself was not so enthusiastic, but he knew that it was too late to turn back, now.

At least he was able to enjoy a good night's rest, for he was not plagued by chilling shrieks or dreadful grins. Instead, he slept soundly until morning.

Ambling into the kitchen to have some breakfast, Dan did not expect to find Miriam and Mr. Flint waiting for him. So, he turned to his employer and asked, "What are you doing, here, Mr. Flint?"

"I came to see you off." said the kindly blacksmith. "I also came to give you this." He handed the boy an elongated and rather crudely wrapped parcel.

Dan accepted the gift from his mentor and carefully removed the wads of cloth. It was a sword, in its own protective sheath – his sword. His very own sword!

"This is unbelievable." Dan breathed.

After eating his breakfast Dan was almost ready to leave. But he had to say goodbye to his father, first.

"In light of the circumstances," the old man began hoarsely, "I see fit to give you a blessing before you go."

Just as he had said this, Miriam entered the room with a shallow bowl of olive oil.

Dipping his thumb into the bowl, Dan's father rubbed the liquid on his son's forehead, lips, and chest. Dan bowed his head solemnly as the man spoke, "May you, Daniel Garnet, use your mind to think pure thoughts; may you use your tongue and your lips to speak them. And may you use your heart to guide your thoughts, your words, and your actions."

When he had finished, Dan lifted his head and turned to leave. But the old man grabbed his hand. "There is one more thing I must tell you before you depart, Daniel." Jonah Garnet looked intently at his nearly full-grown son, and continued gravely, "As you embark on this perilous journey, I beg you to be wary of all the evil forces at work in the world. Beware the forces of Demogorgon; he and his followers will try to prevent you from accomplishing your goal.

"But if you find yourself in trouble, there is hope. For even though Milcham is in bondage, his power can still reach those who seek him."

Dan nodded at the advice.

His father pointed to his nightstand, "Take the pouch with you."

Dan did as he was told. He removed the royal-blue pouch and loosened the drawstrings to open it. Into his hand toppled several chunks of myrrh. "Dad, you need this for the pain." said the boy.

"I can use other remedies for that. I want you to take it with you, and give it to Milcham as a gift when you meet him."

Reluctantly, Dan put the sack away in his pocket. Then, his sister returned to the room. Without warning, she threw her arms around him and hugged him tightly. Planting a kiss on his still-oily forehead, she half-sobbed, "Be careful, little brother."

All too soon, Dan found himself at the top of Citrine Hill, overlooking his village – his home. Taking one last look, he was on his way.

Leaving the huge valley where he lived, Dan trekked through the rolling hills beyond with nothing but a battered, leather cloak wrapped around him. Slung around his shoulder was his bursting-at-the-seams knapsack, which was crammed with all sorts of necessities. From his wiry neck hung King Feldspar's pendant, and from his belt dangled his sword.

Dan hiked for hours on end, following the path of Lapis Creek. It was mid-evening when the young blacksmith finally took a rest stop.

Finding a large pear tree, he sat gratefully under its shady branches.

Absent-mindedly, he unsheathed his sword, glaring with disgust at his unappealing reflection. Once again, he felt doubt creeping into his mind. Dan heaved a huge sigh.

"What's the matter?" asked a friendly voice, from somewhere behind him.

Startled, Dan leapt from the grass, and to his astonishment an enormous salamander emerged from behind the pear tree. "What is troubling you?" the amphibian repeated with a broad grin.

"Get back, beast!" Dan warned with a wave of his new sword.

"Please, don't be alarmed." said the calm, female voice. "I have no intention of harming you."

"Do no lie to me," Dan said, "everyone in the kingdom knows that salamanders are immensely poisonous."

"Alas, that is true." she admitted. "But I promise that I shall never bite you. I merely wish to know what is troubling you."

Dan eyed the creature skeptically. She was gigantic; she could easily overpower him if she desired. But there was something about her that made him trust her. Maybe it was her warm, reassuring smile. "OK." he said at last. "What's your name?"

"My name is Grylio." she replied.

"And I'm Daniel, but I prefer to be called Dan." He said, lowering his weapon. He began to recount all the events of the past few days. He told Grylio everything; he even showed her the necklace that the king had given him. All the while, she listened intently.

Finally, when Dan was finished speaking, she said to him, "I will help you, if you will help me."

"What do you need help with?"

I have longed to taste the fruit of this tree." she responded. "But my feet are too slippery to grasp the fruit, and I cannot bite off the stem, or else the entire tree would whither and die." Grylio explained.

Without hesitation, Dan plucked a pear from a low-hanging branch and tossed it to the salamander.

Grylio took a small sample then, she devoured the rest of the fruit with obvious relish.

Clearly contented after eating, Grylio spoke to Dan as he sat down, again. "So, you say that you are looking for a troll?"

Dan nodded.

"Well," she continued, "I've been traveling in these parts since I was no longer than your finger. And the only troll that I know who lives outside of the Boglands goes by the name of Snorri. He lives in a hidden cave, way up in the Jade Mountains."

"Do you know how to get there?"

"Certainly, but it will be dangerous. And it will take us at least a week to arrive."

"No matter how far it is, I must go." Dan told her. "But it's going to be dark, soon. So, we should not continue until morning."

With that, the boy began to pitch up his tent. As soon as he was done, Dan crawled inside. Weary from his long walk, he fell asleep in minutes. Grylio, however, chose to sleep outside.

The next day, Dan rose just as the morning sun was peeking up from the hills. Grylio was right where he'd left her – curled in a semi-circle near the roots of the pear tree. As far as he could tell, she was still asleep.

Dan washed up in the creek, and made a small fire in order to warm his dry provisions and make some tea. Grylio awakened just as he was removing the small pot from the fire.

She yawned loudly and – to Dan's amazement – walked straight *through* the flames toward him. "Good morning." she said cheerily.

Dan stared at her in awe. "Don't the flames bother you?"

"Oh, no." she said with a smile. "Fire has almost no effect on us salamanders."

Dan ate with his new-found friend, and then they were on their way.

According to Grylio, the fastest path to the Jade Mountains was through the Agate Desert and the Living Forest, two infamous destinations.

As they walked, the scenery changed from green to brown; while the air became hot and dry. They knew that they were entering the desert. The place was arid and desolate; it seemed so empty. A few smooth rocks and towering cacti served as the only landmarks around.

However, the desert was not much of a challenge. For Grylio had devised a clever plan to keep them out of the heat. She proposed that they travel underground.

As they made their way through the tunnel that the salamander was continually digging, Grylio told Dan a bit about her past.

She – like most trolls – had been born in the Boglands. There she had lived with her parents and her 11 brothers and sisters. Their life had been a happy one, until the time of the Troll Revolution. During those days, not only trolls, but all other creatures of darkness had attempted to take over the land. They began first in the Boglands.

Trolls, goblins, and other wicked creatures wiped out Grylio's entire family. Desperately, the girl fled in a passing elf caravan. The compassionate elves took her in and raised her as their own.

"But what ever happened to the Troll Revolution?" Dan had to ask.

"Squabbling among themselves, the various groups disbanded, and the idea of world domination was forgotten." Grylio reminisced, sadly. "Trolls are heartless creatures, and Snorri is even more so. If they were to rise to power like that, again," Grylio shuddered at the thought, "we'd all be doomed. That is why I'm coming with you. I'll help in any way I can to prevent that from happening, and I believe that Milcham is the only one capable of stopping them." she concluded.

Crawling through the tunnel by day and sleeping under the stars by night, in only three days they made it to the edge of the Living Forest.

Grylio gulped audibly as she glared at the dense jungle before them. "I hope you're ready for this." she said in almost a whisper.

"Why do you ask?" Dan wondered aloud.

"They don't call it the Living Forest for nothing."

Now it was Dan's turn to gulp with anxiety yet, putting their fears aside, the pressed onward – into the unknown.

The pair ventured through the thick overgrowth for a total of five days. By the fourth day, they could see the end of the forest, and so far they had not encountered anything potentially dangerous. All they had seen were some mimic insects – which looked too tasty for Grylio to ignore – and a barometz emerging from it's vegetable home. Other than that, there was really much to report.

On their final night in the forest, while Dan was fast asleep in his tent, he began to experience another disturbing nightmare.

In the dream, he was sleeping in his own bed. Then suddenly, out of nowhere, a black, scaly, clawed hand wrapped itself around the boy's neck.

The strangling fist wrenched him from beneath his blankets, and Dan came face-to-face with his attacker. All he saw were two big, orange eyes with slit-like pupils glaring at him, maliciously.

He could not see the beast's mouth, thankfully. But he heard it's booming voice rumbling like thunder. "HOW DARE YOU MEDDLE IN MY PLANS, FOOLISH PEASANT?!" It increased the pressure around Dan's neck and his lungs began to scream for air. "GO TO THE JADE MOUNTAINS, HELPLESS HUMAN," it roared, "AND YOU WILL NEVER RETURN!"

Everything went blank...Then, Dan opened his eyes. Phew! It *was* a dream! He ran a hand gingerly across his neck, trying to convince himself of that.

He glanced around the tent. Right away, he realized that Grylio was gone. She was probably off chasing mimic bugs. He was almost ready to dismiss the thought, when a piercing scream split through the stillness of the night.

Dan rushed outside in a flash, only to find his friend struggling with...a plant? It looked sort of like a Venus fly-trap, though it was much larger. The spiky trap part was closed around Grylio's flank like massive jaws. And what one might have mistaken for leaves acted as arms, pinning the defenseless animal to the ground.

Dan ran to help, at once.

Grylio saw him as she was attempting to bite the overwhelming creature. "I can't... reach!" she gasped. "Cut it!" she yelled to Dan. "Cut it!"

Dan whipped out his sword, and hacked furiously at the thing. But every limb he thought he'd chopped grew back in seconds! His efforts were useless. This plant – or whatever it was – was indestructible.

Grylio continued to yell frantically, "It's *root*! Cut off its root!"

The monster seemed to have understood her, because it lashed out one of its leaves, knocking Dan's sword from his hand. With another swift move, it grabbed the boy's ankle, throwing him to the ground, hard. His weapon was out of reach; there was nothing he could do.

But there had to be something, anything. And there was. But was it even worth a try? Dan had no time to contemplate it. So, he bawled at the top of his voice, "Milcham, MILCHAM!"

Grylio joined him and the two of them continued to cry for help, hoping to be answered.

Just then, Dan glimpsed something moving out of the corner of his eye. It was his sword! It seemed to be drifting toward him of its own accord.

As soon as it was close enough, he grabbed it. And in the blink of an eye, the plant's sole root had been severed. Releasing them both, it crumpled and fell with a dull *thud.*

Still panting from the effort, Dan looked up at the heavens through the canopy of leaves above them and whispered, "Thank you." Then, he turned to his friend to make sure she was all right. Her thick skin was able to withstand most of the monster's strikes, but she did get a small cut on one of her front legs. "Are you OK?" he asked her.

"Yeah." she said. "I'm fine." She waved her leg around to demonstrate.

"So, what was that thing, anyway?" Dan enquired.

"A jidra. The only way to kill one is by slicing off its only root."

After that ordeal with the jidra, the adventurers decided to keep on moving. In mere minutes, they encountered an immensely high wall. They thought they could find a way around it, but there was none in sight. The barrier spread for miles in either direction.

"I guess we'll have to climb it." said Grylio. She gripped the edge of a low, protruding stone and tried to pull herself up, but couldn't. Her cut began to bleed sluggishly.

"Not in *your* condition." the young man objected. "Let me take a look at it." Dan wrapped her wound in a piece of cloth that he had torn from the end of his shirt. He had attempted to apply some myrrh to the wound, but Grylio protested, saying that salamanders were allergic to the resin.

Once her injury was sought after, Dan set to work making a harness. And when that was done, he began to climb the wall.

At the top, he let down the rope and Grylio climbed into the harness. Not putting any pressure on her lacerated leg, the giant amphibian climbed up the wall with much help from Dan, who half-hoisted her. When they landed on the other side, they understood why the Living Forest had been cordoned off.

They had just entered the village of Tourmaline, according to a sign stuck into the dirt just a few feet from the wall. Tacked onto one corner of the wooden greeting sign was a map of the town.

Studying the map with interest, Dan saw an inn located not far from where they were. He also read that there was an apothecary due south. "Take my bag and go to the inn. Pay for a room for us with the change in the pocket." he instructed Grylio. "In the meantime, I'll go to the apothecary and try to find something suitable for your cut." he added.

Dan took some of the money from his backpack before giving it to Grylio. Then, they split up, Grylio with the sack strapped to her back and Dan off to find the medication.

The path to the apothecary's shop led the boy into the heart of town. Soon, the store's sign came into view so, Dan made for it. He was turning out of a side street when he noticed something peculiar.

Outside of a tavern, a man was tethering three horses to a post – two were white, one was black. But there was something oddly familiar about the black horse. And the white ones were selectively bred colts, a fact which was strange in itself. But all became clear when Dan saw who was leading them.

Dan was stunned to see General Percival Quartz leaving the animals and striding into the tavern.

Dan knew that Grylio would be waiting for him, but he just *had* to find out what Percy was up to. So, he pulled his hood over his head and followed the general.

Inside, he found Percy seated at the counter with an untouched pint in front of him. Dan kept his head down and sat at a vacant table in the far corner. From there, he could see and hear Percy without being noticed.

As Dan watched, Percy took a few sips of his drink. He appeared to be completely nonchalant of all the activity surrounding him. The general looked distracted. Someone could have slapped him in the face, and he would not have been aware of it.

He continued to drink airily, ordering another beverage when his first was finished. By the time he was on his third glass, he had attracted the attention of a few of the pub's regulars. He was made numerous offers by people who were interested in buying one of the horses. However, the general refused them all.

Although he was aware of Percy's aggravation, the bartender found it difficult to contain his own curiosity. "You're a knight from Diamond City, aren't you?"

"So what if I am?" Percy questioned.

"It's just – We don't get too many of your type in Tourmaline." the man – who was similar in stature to Percy – said. "If you don't mind me asking – Have you any news from the king's palace?"

"Ha! The king..." Percy laughed. "Yeah, I know some things." he replied to the drink-server. "I can't tell you much, but I *will* tell you this: Old King Feldspar's reign may soon come to a rather abrupt end. His convictions are too weak, and I say it's only a matter of time before he's overthrown by *someone* greater."

Dan had heard more than enough. How could that jerk be so bold and disrespectful to the man he owed everything to?! It was obvious that Percy was not the loyal, patriotic hero everyone thought he was!

Infuriated, the apprentice bolted out of the tavern and onto the dirt road without a second glance. He made a bee-line for the apothecary and stepped inside.

Minutes later, he emerged from the shop, holding a jar of some weird, foul-smelling concoction.

As Dan neared the inn, he saw a large curled mass lying outside the door. To his dismay, he realized that the heap was his friend Grylio. Her eyes glistened with tears as she spoke. "I'm so sorry, Dan." she sniffled. "It's all my fault!"

"What are you talking about, Grylio?" Dan asked, softly. "Where's the knapsack?"

"That's just it!" she wept. "As I was walking to the inn, I was robbed by bandits. There were so many of them I..."

"Calm down." Dan told her. "Did they hurt you?"

The salamander shook her head. "Not really."

At least *that* was good news, Dan thought. But he felt like kicking himself for leaving his injured friend alone.

The thieves had taken everything: their money, their food, their equipment; they even had Dan's spare clothes. "Maybe, if we go in there and explain the situation, they'll let us stay for the night then, in the morning, we could work for our board." Dan suggested.

"I already tried that. And the innkeeper told me to get my venomous hide out of her establishment."

Even after Grylio had told him this, Dan insisted on trying.

"I'm not a charity!" screeched the crabby, old woman behind the check-in counter. "And even if what you and your little friend," she looked contemptuously at Grylio, "say is true, I can't afford to give you a room for free!"

"Please, she's wounded, and I'm willing to work for you as payment." the blacksmith pleaded.

The ill-natured innkeeper merely scoffed and pointed her finger in the direction of the door.

Dan hung his head dejectedly, and the pendant he was wearing slid from underneath his cloak. He and his comrade were about to leave, when the woman called out to them.

"Wait!" she exclaimed, bustling up to Dan and taking hold of the pendant. "This is King Feldspar's crest!" she exclaimed in disbelief. "He sent you, didn't he?"

The apprentice and the salamander nodded simultaneously. "He commissioned me." Dan said.

The innkeeper stood, slack-jawed. Then her mannerism changed at one. "Any servant of the king is welcome, here!"

After having said that, she quickly found them the best available rooms. Then, she ordered her chef to fix them a warm pot of soup. Lastly, she invited Dan to take whatever he needed from her tool shed. And she did all this without making them pay a cent. She also made sure to apologize for the way she had treated Grylio, earlier.

While the two of them were sipping their soup in the dining room, Dan only then remembered the poultice he had bought for the amphibian. He dressed her wound as best as could with it. Then, he went to his room and turned in for the night. But before he did, he gave thanks to Milcham, once again.

Because of all the excitement of the previous night, the pair slept deeply until midday.

Grylio claimed that she was healthy enough to travel. And Dan had to admit that the lumpy mixture had helped her wound improve sufficiently. So, they thanked the innkeeper and her staff before departing.

In the broad daylight, they could see the village clearly, now. However, there was no time for sight-seeing.

The thought of what he had learned about Percy, yesterday, nagged at the back of Dan's mind; though he knew he must continue his mission.

The friends walked to the outskirts of this extremely remote village. They passed the barbed wire fences and warning signs which led to a steep cliff.

From their elevation, they saw a small, wooded area below them and in the distance laid the distinguished greenish-grey peaks of the mountain range they had so tirelessly searched for.

Tying ropes around a nearby tree, Dan and Grylio wasted no time in lowering themselves down the cliff.

The cliff was not as high as they had thought. Once on the ground, they pushed pass the handful of trees and shrubs blocking their path. Then, they were able to behold the remarkable mountains in all their glory.

It was late evening when they arrived at the foot of the mountains.

"Which peak does Snorri live in?" Dan asked.

"His cave is near the middle of the highest peak." Grylio answered.

"So, what are we waiting for? Let's go!" the boy exclaimed.

"Trolls are nocturnal, and it's almost sunset." Maybe, if we wait until morning, we'll be able to sneak in while he's asleep."

The apprentice thought for a moment. "I suppose, we could do that. But Milcham's life is at stake!"

Grylio gasped. "You're right, Dan! We must hurry!" And so began their long, tedious hike. For hours they climbed and climbed, without a moment's rest. In the last rays of the setting sun and in the eerie light of the moon, they journeyed upward.

Several times they heard noises that neither of them had made. But they dismissed any concern when they looked around them and saw no one.

Finally, in the early hours of the morning, they stopped. Hidden between a small crevice, they ate some sandwiches that the innkeeper has sent with them. As they were eating, they heard an unmistakable coughing noise.

Grylio jumped up to see what it was. She peeped over the ledge above them. "There's a man up there." she told Dan.

Dan too, began to peer above the ledge. "That's Percy!" he said to Grylio. "He's King Feldspar's general. But I found out yesterday, that he's disloyal to the throne." he whispered to her.

Together they watched as the general pushed a hidden lever behind a pile of rocks to reveal a door. Leading the horses inside, he followed them. Seconds later, the door slid shut.

Having seen all of this, the friends gathered up their belongings and clambered over the ledge and onto the landing. Imitating Percy's example they were soon inside.

Snorri's lair was exactly the way Dan had envisioned it. It was almost completely dark a few flaming torches provided the only illumination. Dan quickly grabbed one of these, as he and Grylio tried to navigate their way through the cave.

Grylio spoke softly. "I've never actually been in here, so…"

She trailed off when they came across a plunging spiral staircase.

Taking the stairs two at a time, they ran all the way down to what was obviously a dungeon. To the right side, there were two barred cells. One of them contained the skeleton of a large animal. At the far end of the room stood a fireplace, and over the flames hung a large cauldron of bubbling water.

A lone iron cage hung in a corner. In it, the once brilliant bird perched. Naked but for a single tail plume, Milcham's head lolled and his body was motionless. The only indications that he was alive were his unsteady breaths.

Dan and Grylio were heading toward him, when a voice from behind stopped them dead in their tracks. "I knew I smelt some do-gooders!" it said.

They spun around to see Snorri and Percy standing at the bottom of the staircase. Snorri was obviously the one who had spoken.

Before the friends could react, he pulled out a pair of tiny darts, and launched them at the duo. It happened so fast. One second the darts were flying through the air and the next, Dan and Grylio were on the cold, stone floor.

"Take their weapons, would you." the troll instructed Percy. Dan tried to stop him, but his arms felt like lead. He could not budge, or even speak. And neither could Grylio.

Dan slowly began to lose consciousness.

When he awoke, he realized that he was locked in a cell with Grylio beside him. He saw Percy dealing with the troll.

"I'll see you same time next month." Snorri said to Percy, giving him a whole bar of gold.

Dan was appalled at what he was seeing. He summoned all his strength just to speak. "No," he screamed at the departing Percival. "How can you do this?"

Percy paused, but said nothing.

Dan continued to rant, though. "How could you betray your own people, for a sneaky, old troll? Do you think he's going to help you get what you want? How do you know he isn't just using you?"

"That's enough from you, boy!" Snorri threatened. "Percy's on the *powerful* side now!"

When Dan glanced at the doorway, again, Percy was already

gone.

Snorri grinned. "Enough talk. It's time to get down to business. His Wickedness will be here any moment, and I must be prepared."

Dan and Grylio watched fixedly as the troll hobbled over to Milcham's cage and yanked him out. Chuckling sinisterly, Snorri said to him, "I'll ask you one more time just for fun: What is the secret to eternal life?"

Milcham did not answer.

Snorri mocked him, saying, "Some say that the phoenix is immortal. But perhaps he can't reply, because he too, must die!" Slowly, the monster reached over, and pulled out the bird's final feather.

Milcham's eyelids dropped and his body went limp. "No!" said Dan and Grylio, as they watched in horror while the troll put the body back in the cage.

Placing the cage beside their cell, he sneered at them. "Go ahead; mourn for your beloved protector!" With a laugh, he set about preparing his meal.

Dan observed Grylio crying again, and he felt like doing so himself. Milcham had just been murdered, before their eyes. Their journey had been in vain. Worst of all, he might never see his sister or his father, again.

On that note, he remembered the pouch of myrrh in his pocket. Pouring the contents around the lifeless body, Dan said, "I know it's probably too late, but Dad wanted you to have this." Then he and his companion continued to sulk in silence.

Shortly after they had paid their tribute, the crestfallen pair heard a small flapping noise. When they turned to the direction it came from, they saw a tiny bat flutter down from the chimney, through the fireplace and into the dungeon. It alighted on the hard, stone floor. And to their horror, it expanded; shifting it's form from a harmless insectivore into a bloodthirsty gargantuan dragon.

Dan recognized the monster from his last dream.

But it took no notice of him or Grylio. Instead, it focused its attention on Milcham's cage. He thoroughly examined the figure within, as if to make sure that the bird was truly deceased.

With a smirk, the terrifying beast ridiculed the phoenix in his guttural tones. "Why, even the marvelous savior must succumb to the power of death!" he exclaimed. "Now, where is that troll?" he added before he too, mounted the staircase.

Minutes after his departure, the sound of a raucous conversation reached the two prisoners.

"You know who that was?" Grylio asked Dan.

He nodded, and then shivered. "I think I know."

Shh! Keep quiet!

The effects of the darts had already worn off. So, you can imagine how vigorously they jolted at this unexpected voice. "Who's there?" Dan demanded.

It's me, Percy.

Upon hearing this, Dan lunged himself in the direction of the voice. He was ready to strangle that traitor, but Grylio held him back.

"I know you're angry. You have every reason to be." said Percy's voice. "But I'm trying to help you now, so bear with me."

The apprentice was just wondering if the general could be trusted, when the cell door swung open. In seconds, he and his comrade were free from their constrictions.

"I don't really have much time to explain myself," Percy began. But I think that what you said earlier is true and I'm sorry for creating this mess."

Dan was speechless.

Yet, General Quartz kept talking. "Here, eat this. It will make you invisible, like me." Several fern leaves suddenly appeared in front of them.

Without hesitation, the friends ingested the leaves. Now that *they* were invisible, Percy became perceptible to them.

Dan and Grylio were reluctant to leave Milcham's body in that wretched place, but they knew there was nothing they could do about it. So, they followed Percy as he led them out of the dungeon.

Upstairs, they retrieved Dan's sword. Then, Dan and Percy commenced their escape plan by running to the entrance and making a racket. And as planned, Snorri and the dragon stalled their conference to see what all the noise was about. But as the men were invisible, the villains found it difficult to attack.

Unseen, Dan and Percy reined blows on the scoundrels.

Meanwhile, Grylio was trying to get the door open.

Beneath them all, in the dungeon, the myrrh which was surrounding the phoenix ignited, and his body burst into flames.

But up on the main level, the effects of the fern leaves were wearing off. The escapees were slowly becoming visible, again.

The black dragon took this opportunity to release a breath of fire on the two men. But Grylio threw herself in front of them, just in the nick of time.

More out of desperation that skill, Percy tumbled across the floor and kicked at the lever beside the door with all his strength. The boulder slid aside, letting in the first rays of the rising sun.

Snorri tried to make run for it, but he was much too slow. As soon as the sunshine hit him, he shrieked with pain, as his body solidified into stone.

The dragon's attention was diverted for a split-second as he watched his minion's agony. Then – rage renewed – he focused on the threesome.

So, they did their best trying to fend off the monstrous beast. They hit, they sliced, and Grylio even bit. Yet, the dragon stood tall; their volleys did not seem to bother this formidable foe in the least.

Right in the heat of the battle, they all ceased their blows as they saw bright flash of light streak past. Everyone whirled around to see the miraculous form of the golden phoenix, Milcham! He had somehow, resurrected from the dead.

"It can't be!" the giant reptile roared.

The bird spread his vast, shimmering wings and landed at the epicenter of the battle ground. Milcham opened his hawk-like beak and let out a deafening screech.

Clearly conquered, the dragon vanished in a puff of smoke.

Astonished by what had just happened, none of the warriors said anything for quite some time. But they bowed low in respect to the legend.

The silence was broken by the awe-inspiring hero. "I would like to that you, Daniel and Grylio for your faith in me." he commended the duo. "For this, I bestow upon you the gift of everlasting life."

Dan and Grylio exchanged grins.

Percy – on the other hand – looked away from the scene in shame.

Milcham became aware of Percy's discomfort and so, he approached him. "And what do you have to say for yourself, Percival?" he asked gently.

Percy looked from the floor to Milcham's dazzling, hazel eyes. "All I can say is that…that I'm sorry." Percy said in a trembling voice.

Dan had never seen the general so emotion; he actually felt sorry for him.

"Due to your remorse," the phoenix resumed, "you shall have a second chance. However, because of your wrong-doing, you'll find that your days will be a bit more difficult, now. Yet, as long as you believe, you too, will never truly die."

All of this was still so confusing to Dan. "Glorious Milcham, forgive me, but I don't quite understand why everything happened the way it did." said the blacksmith. "Since you're so powerful, why did you allow Snorri to capture and torture you? You could have stopped him."

"Yes, I could have." Milcham answered in his kind voice. "But my fate was already decided since the beginning of time. I had to die physically and then rise to prove that anyone can do so, once they have faith, even if it's just a little." The magnificent bird explained. He addressed both Grylio and Dan, "Is there anything else you would like as a reward for deed?"

Daniel shook his head in humility. In a way, he had already gotten what he wanted. He now knew the answers to the questions he had always pondered.

However, Grylio said that she was tired of people fearing her and her kind. Milcham said he would take care of that. He placed his wing on her head and produced a small corn stalk in mid-air. "Take a nibble at it." he instructed the salamander.

When Grylio did so, she realized that her bite was no longer toxic. Now, there would be no reason for anyone to be afraid of her! Never gain would people run away when she tried to befriend them!

And so there journey concluded. Grylio went back to the Boglands, while Percy and Dan returned home.

When Percy arrived at the palace, he admitted to all his crimes. Naturally, he was demoted from his position as general. But the king chose not to banish him from the empire.

As for Daniel, he made it back to Beryllium with a new lease on life. He saw a spellbinding sense of purpose ahead of him. He was going to spread the good news of Milcham's promise to every living thing with unwavering confidence. The best part of his homecoming: finding out that his father had miraculously been healed of his illness.

What about Milcham? He departed into the heavens the same day that Demogorgon and Snorri had been defeated. But before he left, he warned the trio that their plight was not over. Demogorgon would continue to lurk, until their final confrontation in which all evil would come to an end.

Until then, Daniel, Grylio, Percy, and all others who believe would be ready for anything, because they knew that Milcham was on their side.

Surely, the Gem Kingdom would never forget that. For below the "statue" of Snorri that King Feldspar had erected in Diamond City hung a frame which contained a single gold feather.

The corresponding inscription read:

Our Savior Lives. He Conquers All.

LaVergne, TN USA
30 October 2009

162537LV00001B/40/P